Dream of Angels

&

Other stories

Zaid S Sethi

First published in Hungary by the author 2012, Wesselenyi u.16, Budapest 1077, Hungary

ISBN   978-963-08-3180-2

Printed & bound by
Percprint Nyomdai Műhely
(www.percprint.hu)
Budapest, Hungary 2012

For
Saf & Am,
forever

Contents

Suzi

J

'I promise you Lizzie, I promise I'll bring her back safely.'

She looked at me with her sad eyes as if accusing me of doing something I shouldn't. Sometimes words aren't necessary and although I am no expert on dogs, this one had learned, in the three and a half years that she had lived in our world, that people can be manipulated. It's a very human trait that pets acquire probably through domestication rather than evolution.

The flat was small and tidy. A room full of laundry with its smell of freshly washed clothes, a kitchen with no dishes in the dish rack, and a sitting room with nothing out of place except an abandoned blanket discarded after the comfort of an afternoon nap. The furnishings, though modest, exuded pride in their ability to serve the purpose for which they had been made. I took in the details while in the background Suzi pleaded with her baby.

The flat had warmth that often eludes solitary souls and revealed a wholesome existence of someone who had accepted her lot in life; no longer visibly suffering from the effects of self imposed loneliness. Brightly lit, I noticed the absence of trophies; of memories that accumulate and settle with the dust of time. I could hear Suzi living there, living with Lizzie, someone who could never hold a grudge, never hurt, and quickly overcame the disappointment of mood swings mortals are prone to inflicting on those around them. She had a world the voyeur in me delighted in.

'She's like an only child, jealous of strangers.'

The terms of endearment Suzi used made me smile as if somehow I wanted to share in that affection and, at the same time, imagined what it must be like to be in Lizzie's place; to be betrayed with such kindness. I let Suzi say her reluctant good-byes, watching her coax Lizzie into a basket placed just outside her bedroom.

'Does she really sleep in her basket?'

'Only during the day,' she smiled, as if letting me into a secret she wasn't sure she knew me well enough to share. I smiled too. I imagined Lizzie lying close to her, wondering whether it would be skin she felt or a night suit, 'but at night, well...' A little laugh left out the unnecessary detail.

Suzi completed her good-byes and we left.

♪♪

I had known Suzi for about four months before I asked her out. I persuaded myself that it wasn't a date because of the casual manner in which I had asked whether she would like to meet up for a drink. I imagined at best it would be one evening after work but, when in reply to what might be a good time she suggested a Saturday evening I was pleasantly surprised. She said it would have to be about nine o'clock in the evening because she had to take her dog out for her evening walk. I said that wouldn't be a problem but, in deference to my greed, asked whether I could join her for the walk as well. We arranged to meet at six.

The evening walk in the park near her flat was pleasant although, with Saturday night on the horizon, couples were setting the scene with romantic posturing; the holding of hands, the clinging of ownership and studied kisses that disturbed the rustle of the trees with noisy togetherness. We talked little during the walk and, when we did, it wasn't strained conversation, more a comfortable feeling of a couple that had either moved beyond indulgent beginnings or still wrestled with the uncertainty of what the future might hold.

Walking back to her flat I felt a little sad that at 8pm the evening was already drawing to a close. The walk in the park left me uncertain of what should happen next. After some hesitation I took my chance and asked her whether she would like to have dinner. No, Suzi didn't eat after 6 pm. Coffee didn't work either because she didn't drink coffee. I was persistent. Tea and cake at a tea house nearby? That didn't work either because she didn't like sweets. I had run out of ideas and resigned myself to enjoying the last remaining moments of the evening.

'I could come for a drink?'

'That would be nice,' I said, containing my excitement.

'We have to drop Lizzie off first.'

We dropped Lizzie off at her flat despite the mongrel's protests and walked to a café Suzi liked a block away.

11

Suzi was in her late twenties. I assumed from the fact that she was free on a Saturday evening that she wasn't in a serious relationship. I knew that was an assumption that couldn't be relied upon but, for the moment, it seemed enough. Her hair, shoulder length, was tied back with a neatness that was repeated in the way she dressed. She had obviously spent time on her make-up which continued the completeness of the style she had chosen. Jeans folded up to reveal boots snugly tied around her ankles. No jewellery, no watch, and nails polished with a discrete shade of nothing in particular allowed no jarring of colour across her fingers. Sitting opposite her in the café I was given the opportunity to notice details previous casual meetings had not allowed which delighted me with an intensity sweet for a first meeting.

There was something about being surrounded by people that allowed the conversation to flow more easily though, in my exuberance, I missed questions I would have liked to ask. The sort of questions that, with the moment having been lost, meant they could never be asked, or if asked, could never be answered. These were questions that didn't mean much out of context, but over time would assume an importance in my mind beyond what is generally accepted as normal.

We talked about our lives before we met; loves lost and lovers forgiven. The abstract questions and answers in our quest for love attempted definitions that countless before us had tried and failed. It was a lost cause and we knew it, but even so we struggled to express ourselves during what ended up being nothing more than taking part in the mating game. The openness of our conversation troubled me as I, at each interlude, tried to take stock of where the conversation was going. I had no plans to sleep with her and therefore the aim of the male in me didn't play an important part in the exchange, nor did it inspire the direction of the conversation. It was as if neither of us cared about the answers except for the struggle to be honest, an honesty of strangers that led nowhere.

It was a long drink without the relaxation of alcohol and it was a surprise again that time passed effortlessly. The atmosphere was of quiet conversations and we took part in the group therapy provided by those around us in the cafe. Normally a change of scene would have helped but, without the excuse of thirst or hunger, the evening seemed destined to revolve around conversation.

'Do you like sleeping alone?'

The question appeared without warning. I tried to relate it to the context of what went before. I couldn't. I concentrated on the question to prevent my imagination running away with me. I had noticed her physical appearance with the eyes of a predator and, having satisfied myself that it was a body that was formed well enough to provide physical pleasure, had moved on to other subjects. I was not hunting. I hesitated for a moment trying to understand whether there was something I had failed to notice and then answered truthfully.

'No, I don't.'

'Then why have you chosen to live the way you do?'

I was in my forties; successful enough to think about investments rather than whether I had enough to live on. A failed relationship and several false starts had left me looking for what in normal circumstances would be hard to find; a relationship that could be guaranteed not to fail, particularly as time was running out. The normal routine of attraction, desire, contentment and ambivalent affection, the cycle I was always looking to break despite seeing it all around me. I wanted something more. I say something more as I was sure there was something beyond the superficial love stories, romantic songs or plays that tormented audiences with the artistic emptiness of broken relationships. I wanted something once, something that lasts forever, with the passion of being the first to want it and then, like all those that had gone before me or live in the parallel lives that surround us, I fell into the trap of being impatient.

'I don't know.'

It was the truth. I didn't really know why my former relationships had failed. Perhaps the initial feeling transformed itself into the illusion of what I wanted to see. The mirage where lungs fill with sand despite the taste of water, and the slow incredulousness of realising that death comes to dreamers in many guises. Like fools gold, everything attracts the animal, with the power of possession, the pleasure of conquest as proof of self worth, the boredom of achievement and the self pity of loss, all together continue to preach the attractive religion of inner peace.

My uncertain reply ended that line of questioning. I wanted to know the answer myself and was disappointed that Suzi had given up so soon. I wanted her to probe. She had started something and I wanted her to continue. There were too many questions that had arisen in my life which I had parked in the subconscious mind, all with the hope that someday, an event, a moment, an angel of mercy, something, anything, would trigger the senses to allow the indulgence of latent memory and, the awakening, my awakening, would come with an answer to the question. In triumph, I would then discard it as unimportant and move on to the next great unanswered question in the same way great mysteries seem to lose their significance once they have been resolved.

'I don't think it was a conscious decision. It just seems to have turned out that way.'

Suzi seemed to be struggling too.

'You know, when I was young, my sister had a boyfriend. I liked him and thought how wonderful it would be if he would marry my sister. My sister and I were not that close, but close enough for me to want her to find someone I liked too so that we would still be able to enjoy the filial relationship our parents had given us. He spoilt it all by telling me he was in love with me. I couldn't be the same with him after that. He died in an accident. I wondered all these years whether it would have made any difference if I had accepted his love.'

Suzi seemed to recount the events as if they had happened recently. She was looking at me as she told me the story but her eyes, those beautiful grey eyes cradled in the sea of white, seemed distant. I listened to her story with the general interest that it required, enjoying the moment to look at her face, taking in all that I had so much wanted to see, but not until that moment had been given the opportunity.

It was different when she recounted the story of her past loves. They sounded like stories from a newspaper told by a journalist who knows of the numbness of his readers to factual accounts of disaster. There was nothing sensational about them. For some reason old lovers never find their place in histories that can be retold.

'I didn't realise what it meant until I saw him in a dream. I knew he was dead and asked him what he was doing in my dream. I asked him whether I could have prevented his death with the sacrifice of a sister. The dream was recent. He told me something that made me realise that the meaning of his death was not part of my life.'

I asked Suzi what he had told her. She hesitated. It was as if I had asked her something that I shouldn't have asked. Her face struggled to contain the pain in her eyes. I apologised and asked her to forget the question.

'No,' she said, 'I can't remember what he said. I've been struggling to remember because it was so important to me at the time. It's only been two weeks since the dream last recurred and I've never been able to remember what he told me.'

I wondered whether she was exaggerating the importance of an event for dramatic effect just as in the same way newspapers resort to sensationalist remarks to interest the reader. I looked for some evidence in her behaviour, but all I could find was a silent expression of pain.

'Did you love him?'

16

Another question I shouldn't have asked. It was too late to retract it.

'No, I don't think I did.'

It was not the answer I expected because experience had shown that in those moments just before nakedness, whether it is the soul or the physical body that is to be left unprotected, most people try to hang on to the illusion of modesty. Artists have depicted that moment with repetition, whether it was Eve at the fall or Suzanna with the elders. It would have been too easy to say she had loved him.

'You know, I don't really know. Maybe I did.'

I suppose that's what I found interesting in Suzi. She was a soul mate, someone who was struggling as I was, and perhaps countless others, determining the truth about our emotions, the futility of the struggle never discouraging us.

'Do you think truth exists?'

That was a good question for which I had a stock answer, but again it would have been too easy. I wanted her to fall into the trap she had laid out for me.

'What do you think?'

'I don't think it does. It's whatever you choose it to be. After all, reality is perception isn't it?'

I ignored the question which I decided was rhetorical anyway. It was her voice that drew me to her. Soft, lower than usual, and the hesitant thoughtfulness with which she chose her words made her attractive. I liked the way her lips carefully framed the sounds before she let them pass. She noticed me staring. I recovered with a camouflage...

'Actually I don't agree. Reality exists in spite of perception. If the sun is shining it is light despite a blind man's perception that it is dark.'

She looked disappointed at the game I had started playing with her but then, almost immediately, let the disappointment pass and smiled.

Yes, it was those lips that I had noticed the very first time I had seen her. Lips that could form a smile that forgave insensitivity.

'You know, you have a beautiful voice.'

She smiled again.

'You like to surprise don't you?'

'Why do you say that?' I asked.

The waiter intruded with the familiarity of an old friend.

'Can I get you something else?'

'I'll have another drink.'

Suzi didn't want anything. It was getting late and I knew that time was running out. I would soon be walking home alone with the white noise of the city in my ears. There were only two alternatives that I could see; to go home with Suzi and fumble the sort of conclusion that only inspires regret or, go home on my own enjoying the pain of having delayed the end.

Her phone rang.

'Please do answer it.' I said, as I got up to leave to allow some privacy. She looked at the phone and switched it off.

'Why did you do that?'

'I know who it was and I don't want to speak to them now. I'm enjoying spending the time with you.'

18

I thanked her silently although I wondered who it had been. Was I now intruding?

I looked at Suzi's face again. How I wanted to paint it if I could paint. Take a photograph home with me. Stay in this café and let life pass us by, frozen in marble. Not as great sculpture, more like chocolate box depictions of mediocrity. I wouldn't mind. It would be us that would be important and not the adoration of strangers. I suddenly felt the burden of the constant movement that living demands of us. Perhaps that is the truth that the constellations reveal each night as they sail across the sky.

Her eyes showed signs of tiredness that her make-up had given up trying to hide. I remembered seeing the anti-aging creams in a chemist and wondered why it was that women were so concerned about hiding those signs of aging, an endearing quality that comes from giving up the struggle to attract when one has found another human being to trust.

God, those eyes! They were so beautiful! I felt a little foolish because here I was wasting the opportunity of going in for the kill and, instead, delighting in the pleasure of beauty.

'What are you thinking about?'

'Nothing.'

'I think you must be tired.'

Suzi laughed. 'Why, does it show?'

'A little.'

'I don't think I am.'

She was lying. Her politeness indicted I had carried this on too long.

'Come on, it's time to take you home,' I said.

I got the bill. Suzi got her coat and scarf and I let her pass in front of me.

As I turned to follow her I noticed a solitary man sitting at the table behind us nursing a beer. His eyes followed Suzi walking up the stairs. I knew what he was thinking. I smiled to myself.

'Yes,' I thought, 'you're right. Thanks for reminding me.'

* * *

The Affair

'You know, you really ought to stop saying things like that.'

'What?'

'What you just said.'

'What did I just say?'

'Stop doing that.'

'What?'

'Saying all those things.'

'Are you flirting with me?'

'No, I think I'm falling in love.'

'Don't be silly.'

'No really. I think I am.'

'That's silly. I'm married.'

'I know. So am I.'

The telephone rang just in time to reinforce what she was saying. She looked at the number.

'Sorry, it's my daughter.'

'No, please take it.'

She smiled at me as she took the call. She spoke for a while with tenderness and then instruction.

'Fifteen years olds can be so demanding,' she said, as put her phone away in a hand bag that bore no resemblance to the femininity she exuded.

'What were we talking about?'

'Nothing really.'

'Oh yes, I remember. It was something about love.'

'You see, *you* are the one that's flirting.'

She laughed as she picked up her glass of wine and took a sip, but her eyes didn't leave me throughout the performance. When she felt she had done enough, she replaced the glass on the table with theatrical finesse.

'Women have the right to flirt too,' she said.

'Yes, I know, especially married women!'

'And married men!'

We both laughed as if, in the game we were playing, we were now even.

I think I know why we met and it wasn't only for the pleasure of flirting. There was an attraction. In fact I noticed it from the very first moment I saw her. It is easy to notice these things because they are less frequent that we like to think. But I was not kidding when I said that I thought I was falling in love. It was an innocent betrayal for which I could forgive myself. After all we were two married people with a legitimate excuse to meet, knowing full well that at the end of it we could go home to our respective partners in a state of light headed absolution.

The meal was almost as good as the wine and the afterthought of ordering dessert was only to prolong the evening. Coffee was not necessary as the bottle of wine was still half drunk. I knew we should think about stopping because no matter how innocent everything was going to be, we would still need the presence of mind for explanations when we got home. That is the problem of sharing a bed. No amount of washing gets rid of the smell of guilt.

There was another call. This time it was her son. At seventeen years old he was still enjoying the pleasure of being a child.

'Sorry, it's my son.'

It wasn't really an apology. The first time I suppose it could have been, but this time she was showing off. She might as well because I know doesn't last forever. My son stopped engaging me when he was sixteen.

It was as if she had read my thoughts.

'It's different for fathers. There is an air of competition that settles in and fathers can't always cope. I know my husband already shows signs of disaffection.'

She may have been right but it was not exactly what I wanted to talk about. We had been having dinner for nearly two hours and we had spent at least half that time talking with pride about our children and the rest about our other halves. I wanted to hear about her. As those thoughts passed through my mind, I realised that she *had* actually been talking about herself. Her children, her husband and her work were all things that defined her as a person.

'So what do you love?'

'My children.'

'What do you like about your work?'

'It helps, so that together my husband and I can manage the household budget. Teenage children are expensive. They want to follow friends or brands. I like the challenge of work. It makes me feel as if I am doing something useful.'

I felt useful once. Now everything was a routine. We didn't even have rows anymore. It's not that I enjoy rows but, on reflection, they provide, in a somewhat perverse way, a conduit for the passion we need to make relationships work.

'My husband tries his best and he appreciates my contribution.'

I know I should have concentrated on what she was saying rather than looking at her lips, her mouth, the almost invisible pendant hiding indiscreetly in her blouse, the lack of ear rings and all the other things that exuded confidence in her state of being. I thought of what I might do if we had an affair.

'You know you said you were falling in love with me?'

'Yes.'

'Well, what did you mean, exactly?'

How do you answer a question like that? It was long past the time that we should have been in bed having sex rather than wasting time talking about something that would soon exhaust us, leaving us unfit for anything else.

'You know, love isn't something that you should talk about seriously. Falling in love is a dangerous game to play when you are married.'

'You've become very sensible all of a sudden,' I said.

'I think one of us should.'

'No, I think that is more dangerous if Hollywood is to be believed. Let's just joke about it. After all, isn't that one of the few pleasures that married people can have.'

I could tell the waitress had already assumed we were lovers, or about to become lovers, and looked past us with obvious boredom. I wonder whether it was the monotony of seeing concentrated insincerity each evening that made her maudlin about the way she served us or whether she still had the hope, though fading, that there was something real out there. I didn't hear a sound but felt her presence; quiet and deliberate, so that when we had tired of this charade and she was noticed again, she could offer a practiced smile.

'But tell me, what if we weren't married, what would you do?'

That was the cue I was waiting for. Nothing allows us more pleasure than engaging in questions of 'what if?' What if I could start all over again? What if I was single? What if I was a millionaire? What if she was young and innocent? So many 'what ifs?'

It was like playing 'what ifs' with imaginary friends. I had watched my little sister, an afterthought of parents that had married young, do that with natural ease. There was no sense of having to try. She would be watching television one minute with the rest of us and the next minute start a quiet conversation of her own with...I can't remember whom.

'Shh, they will hear us,' my sister would say and we would start to whisper listening to the one sided conversation.

Sometimes Mum would break the spell by asking her who she was talking to and that would end it. Her friends were shy. They didn't like grownups. Grownups frightened them. If Mum persisted she would run off crying into another room. I would go after her and hold her in my arms telling her not to cry, promising her that everything would be alright. 'Tell them not to be frightened,' I would say. She would tell them and give me a kiss of thanks from an imaginary friend. I would wonder what they would be like if they were real and what if I could see them, too?

'I don't know?' I said, giving the impression that I had been thinking about it, 'what would you do?'

She looked at me as if my answer annoyed her, but then her expression changed; a mischievous smile appeared and she blew me a kiss.

'That's what I would do,' she said.

'I would kiss you too.'

'But what if I wasn't ready for a kiss? What if told you that I'd never been kissed?'

'I would know that you were lying but I wouldn't say so.'

I noticed her hands clasped together; right over the left, hiding her tell tale ring. Her skin was no longer the taut skin of youth. The veins undulated on the back of her hand as if they mapped a barren landscape scared by dark hills. I looked up and saw her looking at me as if waiting for me to say something. She arched her eye brows encouraging me to continue. Dark eyebrows, a darker shade of brown than her hair showing off the better care her hairdresser gave her than she managed on her own. Her eyes were set quietly away from high cheek bones. Still confident of her ability to be attractive, they sparkled with adolescent excitement.

I thought of my family; my children, my wife who had long ago given up any hope in instilling in me the comfort of being at peace with everything they tried so hard to offer. I thought of what they must be doing. My wife would have chased my youngest away from the television to her bed with stern unequivocal commands, and the older two would be busy in their rooms, hopefully doing some homework. I wondered why I was here having dinner with a happily married woman in a friendship that had blossomed from a surreptitious exchange of e mails related ostensibly to work. What was I trying to achieve? Was it to betray my family, give up everything that I had worked for or, was it to rekindle excitement without the desperation I had when there was no comfort of having a family to look after me when it all went wrong. But then again, I had the same questions for her, and it was as if knowing she was guilty of the same crime I felt absolved; as if the guilt we both shared was enough to negate any personal reprimand that we deserved.

'Why did you want to see me?'

'Because you are beautiful,' I lied. I know it was a lie because I didn't have a reason to give. The truth was that I hadn't thought about it. I don't think we think through these things; they just happen. Events simply follow one after the other like a ball rolling along after the first gentle push, gaining momentum before gravity and friction slow it down. The metaphor is apt because like the ball you never end up where you started.

'You are very good. I'm sure you do this with every woman you meet.'

Shall I deny it? Shall I admit that I don't do this very often? Shall I say there was something about her that inspired me more than all the others that might have done in my life or, shall I simply accept it as a compliment no matter how undeserved it was.

'You are the first.'

'You are lying.'

I wish I was. I wish I could justify the title of gigolo that she wanted to give me, but the truth is that this was unusual. At least I hope it is unusual. I hope it is because if it is not then there is a universal sadness that permeates the world.

'How's the dessert?' I asked.

'Sweet.'

I smiled at her cleverness.

'Would you like to try some?'

She scooped a piece of her soufflé, drowning her fork in the chocolate sauce before holding it above her plate, pointing it towards me. I accepted the intimacy of eating from her fork and moved forward wrapping my lips deliberately around the fork, taking the offering. I stared at her as I let the chocolate melt in my mouth. She stared back.

I played with the morsel as if it were her tongue, imagining her eyes closing involuntarily as mine would, savouring the moist aphrodisiac that our combined effort would create. She smiled at my exuberance and I returned the compliment. She broke the spell by looking at her watch. I looked at my watch too. It should have been later than 9 o'clock if it's true that time passes quickly when you are having a nice time.

'What time do you have to be home?'

'It's ok; I'm not in a rush. Are you?'

I was never in a rush. My wife had become used to me getting home late. It would just be another long day at work. She would have eaten. The children would have finished for the evening and I would wash, change and go to bed to get ready for another long day at the office.

'No, I'm OK too.'

I wondered how much more preparation we would need to make the evening complete, if complete meant what the evening could be leading up to.

'Do you wonder what life would have been like if it had been different?' I asked.

'No, I'm happy with the way things have turned out. Are you?'

'Yes, I am. I think I have everything I ever wanted.'

'Yes, me too.'

I want to think that we were both lying because it was convenient to lie. Truth is often exhausting.

'But I do think you are beautiful.'

She blushed.

'You're just saying that.'

The denial was involuntary.

'It's a pity that we can't indulge in a romance,' she said dropping the disguise we develop as we gain in experience.

'Why not?'

'Because we are married!' she said, as if losing patience with my childishness.

'I'm sorry.'

'That's ok,' she said, not entirely convinced she should forgive me.

'No really, I'm sorry.'

'It's ok; I ask myself the same question. We have one life and the experiences we allow ourselves somehow don't seem to be enough. We build cages in which we live because without them we are frightened that we wouldn't survive.'

'I think that fear is fortunate. We can't really survive without the comfortable environment we create for ourselves no matter how courageous we think we might be.'

The intrusion of reality, of two married people having dinner, dampened the flirtatiousness of the earlier part of the evening. It was time to go.

'Shall we?'

'I suppose so.'

There was a reluctance to end the evening. I was disappointed that the conversation had taken the direction it had, but couldn't think how the honest affection I think we clearly had for each other could have allowed for anything else. I looked for the bored waitress and, after an aborted attempt or two, got her attention and the bill.

I offered her my hand walking out of the restaurant which she took as we stepped into the street. It was a momentary relapse because she withdrew it almost immediately, but it was still long enough to sense the tenderness I had imagined over dinner. It was a beautiful summers' evening made more beautiful by all the things I was feeling. I didn't want it to end but was reconciled to my fate of leaving everything else to imagination.

'Where's your car?' I asked.

'Around the corner, a street away.'

'I'll walk you to it, it's a lovely evening,' I said, and we walked the hundred yards or so to the street corner where we would turn to find her car.

'It is beautiful, isn't it? Shall we walk for a bit?'

'Yes, lets,' I said, pleased that she had offered.

We walked along the road away from where her car was parked. We turned a corner off the main road into a tree lined avenue lined with Victorian Mansions and struggling street lights. A chill in the air brought her closer to me and we accidentally brushed against each other. We apologised without words.

'It was a lovely dinner.'

'Thank you,' I said, 'I enjoyed it too.'

The darkness gave me courage as I looked for her hand. She was tentative at first; withdrawing her hand again as soon as they touched, but then she changed her mind and gave me her hand. I acknowledged the gesture with a smile of reassurance and felt her hand relax in mine.

We were, however, far from relaxed. We walked hand in hand as if we were teenage lovers worried about being seen by unkind friends or acquaintances; worried that if we looked at each other, others would see us too. We walked along without feeling the need for conversation and, pleasant as it was, soon turned the corner into the street where her car was parked. I don't know whether it was the thought of the evening coming to an end, or whether I could contain myself no longer, but I stopped. She looked at me as if to ask if everything was alright. I looked at her and, after coping with childlike hesitation, we kissed.

It is strange why, in the moment of what cannot be denied to be a betrayal of the lives we lived, there was not sufficient guilt to stop us doing what we were doing. It was as if the world we came from somehow disappeared, melted into the distance beyond the trees, into the safe flats that looked discreetly inwards, giving up the views that had helped sell them in the first place. We kissed as if that is what we had meant to do all evening, but did so with trepidation. It was a brief kiss, but was long enough for us to understand something had happened. We barely managed to say goodbye, walking away from each other as if nothing had been lost and we were respectable again.

*   *   *

John, Carroll & me

There was John, Carroll and me. We met because there was something important to discuss. We met at The Nag's Head; a pub where we discussed matters of life and death ever since we were at school. They were things that were important and needed to be discussed like what job we were going to get, who we were seeing, who we were going to marry, what we were going to name our children, what car we were going to get and other important things like that.

Our wives were busy at home putting the children to bed while the three of us met to discuss things that were important. Important things, you know, I just told you, something important.

Anne has made a face or two when I said that I was going out to meet John and Carroll. She always did. She didn't like them. Never did. I said I'd be home in time and winked as I left.

'In your dreams!' she said, but I knew better. Anne wasn't like Edith.

Carroll's wife, Edith, called him a drunken slob when he got home late, but he didn't mind. He always said that he knew he was and left it at that. She said that he snored like a pig when he'd been drinking and he said he knew. Carroll said that he wasn't as daft as the rest of us to go arguing with his wife.

And that left John. He was getting a divorce so that was alright. His wife had left him because she said she realised she couldn't stand him. She didn't mind the money though. He was

33

upset, was John. He called her names and we told him that wouldn't help. He said that he wanted to bash her head in, but we told him that would cost extra, so he didn't. She took the kids too, but all that was decided a long time ago so I didn't know what we were going to talk about.

We got there at eight. John was already there and had had a few drinks to get warmed up.

'Good,' he said seeing me come in, 'your round.'

Carroll came in as I was getting the drinks so I got him one too. As we huddled around the table John was playing with a beer mat, staring at his beer.

'So,' I said, 'what's happened?'

'Nothing.'

I'd told Anne that we had to meet up because there was something important and now John was saying that he had nothing to say! That wasn't very helpful. I mean, just because he screwed up his own marriage that was no reason to screw up ours. He better say something or else!

'What do you mean, 'nothing!''

'She wanted the house.'

'The bloody house!'

'She said she'd go to Court if I said no.'

'Bloody hell!'

'Her solicitor said I'd lose because of the children, but mine said it wasn't a done deal. It doesn't matter. I've decided to let her have it anyway.'

'You what!' I shouted.

I knew there was something important to decide. We had to decide whether John was an idiot and deserved what he got or, whether there was still a chance that he might save something. Anne said John deserved what he got, but she didn't like him. She never did.

'I thought you wanted to bash her head in!'

'Yes I did. But you know...the children and all that. She'd have made it difficult for me to see the kids. She said that I could have some money to put down as a deposit on a new house and, she wouldn't ask for alimony.'

'Now that makes sense, you cretin! She earns more than you do anyway.'

I was getting angry and the flat beer wasn't helping much. I decided to drink it down so I could get a fresh one.

Carroll wasn't angry. He never got angry, the Moron! I mean you should see the way Edith treats him. I once asked how he manages to put up with her and he said it was easy. He said he just didn't argue with her. He couldn't see the point of having an argument when he would still have to get into bed with her. I mentioned the couch, but he said that no matter how many days he slept on the couch he would still have to get in bed with her sooner or later, so why bother. I didn't tell him that I thought she looked like a dog and I wouldn't get into bed with her if I were blind drunk and she were the last woman on the face of this earth. His kids were alright though. Don't know how, they didn't look a bit like her.

'OK, whose round is it?'

Carroll got the round in. John was still staring at the beer mat or his beer which had died a long time ago.

'Has it all been settled?' asked Carroll.

'Well, I think so. The lawyers talk about a lot of stuff that doesn't make sense. I asked mine afterwards what happens now. He said, if I didn't want to fight it, he would have to have separate discussions with her lawyer to find out how to settle everything legally.'

'That just means that he's mad at you because they aren't going to make as much money out of you lot. Don't worry, they'll find a way to make sure they don't lose out.'

'You know, you're a cynical bastard.'

'Listen, I'm your mate. I don't like it when some bloody lawyer takes my mate for a ride.'

I know I'm right. I'm always right when it comes to telling others what a mess they are making of their lives. I don't complain about mine. You never get me complaining. I mean, there isn't anything to complain about. Anne is ok. She's no beauty which means she's grateful for what she's got; me and two kids. I've got a job and, apart from meeting Carroll and John for a drink once in a while, I don't go out much. Anyway, it's good to help. I mean, if you looked at it from where I'm sitting it's really weird that everyone has problems. Anne and I have our rows but they don't last long; a few doors slammed, a couple nights on the couch and everything back to normal. I mean, you'd have to be a mean bastard not to realise that the kids don't enjoy us having a row that drags on. I know they could've been avoided but you don't really think about that at the time, do you?

Carroll was OK. He had realised that he was a weak bastard and so it was best that he keep his mouth shut. Everyone said he was a wimp, but he didn't mind because as he said 'sticks and stones.' I didn't respect him much, but he was a friend. You don't have to agree with the way friends live their lives because you don't have to live with them. All you have to do is deal with them in between drinks and, so long as the beer isn't flat, it's easy to cope.

Carroll didn't say much about what was happening with John. He grunted a few time and when I asked him to say something he would say, 'Hmm, well, that's a tough one!'

We had all given up on pushing Carroll into taking sides in any discussion. He never offered an opinion. He always agreed.

'John, you're mad. I think you should fight the bitch. She doesn't deserve what you're giving her.'

'Yeh, I know, but I am not giving her anything. She's taking it,' John said quietly, downing the rest of his beer.

'Bloody hell, John, where is the man I knew who wanted to bash her head in!'

'Well, you said it wasn't worth it.'

He had a point. We told him there wasn't much point. He was getting access and she didn't want any alimony.

'So what happens now?' asked Carroll.

I was just going to ask the same question.

'Well, I have to wait. I mean, I can stay in the house. She said that would be alright.'

'That's rich!' I said.

'She wanted to come round to get some things for the children and I said that was alright. I told her solicitor that she could come during the day while I was at work. She's still got a key.'

'And you're not going to be there?' I asked. I mean what if she took other stuff. Like, for example, John's stuff. I mean she could take the lot and he wouldn't be able to prove that she didn't. I mean, God! Some people are really stupid. I mean, don't get me wrong, I really like John, but my God, he's really stupid sometimes.

John drank his beer. I suppose I shouldn't have been so hard on him. After all, I suppose with what he was going through he couldn't be expected to think clearly, but, at the time, I wasn't thinking clearly either.

'John, are you listening to me?'

He just looked at his beer. I don't know why but his silence made me mad. I mean, what do you when your friend's behaving like an arsehole! There's you trying to help and all he does is look at you as if he's some kind of moron.

'Jesus, John, it's your life! Shit, I know what I'd do in your place, but it's your bloody life.'

'Oh, shut up.'

Can you believe it? Carroll told me to shut up. There he is, saying nothing and, when he opens his mouth, he tells me to shut up. I can't believe this guy. I could have been at home giving Anne one! Instead, I come out to see my friend who needs my help and doesn't understand a word I'm saying, and then there's Carroll who tells me to shut up. I was so mad, I can tell you. I got up and went to the loo, just for something to do. I sat there in the cubicle until some idiot started banging on the door. I am glad I went in before he did. He looked desperate!

I came out, washed my hands and splashed water on my face. The dryer wasn't working so I had to wipe my face on my sleeves. I felt a little better. When I went back into the bar I couldn't see Carroll. John was still there looking at his beer. He looked up at me.

'Where's Carroll?' I asked.

'He's gone.'

'Gone where?'

'Gone.'

'John, this isn't a guessing game. Where's he gone?'

'I don't know. He just said he'd had enough and left.'

At the time we didn't realise what happened that night. I mean, we thought Carroll had just got the hump and gone home.

Carroll left home that night. Carroll, who wouldn't say 'boo to a goose', left Edith after living with her for eleven years. He let Edith keep the house and the children. Edith wanted to see him, but he said that he didn't want to. Edith got mad; tried to sue him for alimony and deny him rights to see the children. His solicitor arranged it so that she kept the house and children but no alimony. I don't know how he managed to do that because I thought you always got alimony if your wife wanted it. I mean, the children were still young.

I don't really understand what the hell happened to him. He gave up his job and moved south. I think he lives somewhere in London. I don't know for sure as he's never rung. We'd been friends since school and the bugger just disappeared on us. I didn't see John again either. He rang once. I think it was from Sheffield or somewhere like that.

I talked to Anne about it, but she never liked my friends. She said I was mad to hang around with that sort and, seeing what happened to John and Carroll, I suppose I am. I mean, Anne and I have a family. Yeh, true, we row once in a while but nothing serious. I call her a cow, she calls me a pig, and then we make up. I never understood why John and Carroll didn't ever learn. I mean, I must have told them a hundred times. I'm good at giving advice, but sometimes you can't get people to listen and then what happens, they just go and screw up their lives, don't they?

*   *   *

Wasteland

I slept in my bed, alone, the taste of the gutter in my mouth. It had been a sad day, one of many, but I wanted for nothing. You were by my side but wouldn't allow me to touch you and, then left as quietly as you had appeared. I was sick. First, in my stomach and then in my mouth, the mouth you kissed, the mouth in which you left the taste of the gutter. It was all born of loneliness, this feeling. I saw you in that loneliness as you struggled to sleep, struggled to put out of your mind all the strange experiences you inhaled during the day, snoring a lullaby without words.

I was sitting in a cemetery leaning on a tombstone thinking of you. My heart sank as my memory of you faded.

He appeared as shadows played hide and seek in the sun light. A photographer without a name came to join me. He sat down beside me and shared my wine. He was alone too, but had stories to tell. He didn't mind my smell. Maybe I was interesting. He thanked me for the wine and, in return, offered me a story. A story told in photographs without the commentary of clever people. I wiped the vomit from my mouth on my sleeve, took a drink from the bottle, wiped my mouth again, passed the bottle to him and listened.

There was once a boy who didn't want to be born, sent out into the world before his time. His mother nursed him. She desperately wanted him to survive. It wasn't her first but she wanted it to be the first that she wouldn't lose.

He took another swig from the bottle and passed it to me. He said the wine was good. He said it tasted like death. I knew what he meant as I had tasted death. I told him. He laughed. I laughed too.

He grew up to be a normal child but retained the fear with which he was born. The fear of being thrown into the world all alone, with nothing to help him survive except the love of the woman responsible for bringing him into this world, the woman who taught the child to call her mother. I was that child.

The wine worked its' magic. He was not talking to me anymore. He said the story didn't have to be mine. He would throw it in my direction leaving me to decide whether I wanted it. I could pick it up if I did.

I looked at his face again. It was old. His camera slung over his shoulder rested on the ground beside him. The earth was cold and the grass moist. It must have been the dew. The morning crept out of the earth secretly. I didn't see it come. You didn't either because you weren't there. My trousers soaked up the dew.

I learned to love her as she taught me. She told me she loved me. She did things for me, and told me all the things she'd done for me as reasons why I should love her. I learned to love people who do things for you. I learned that to be

42

the only truth. I promised I would live by that principle which made her happy.

I smiled because I knew that principle too. I'd heard it somewhere. Perhaps it was from my mother too. Perhaps that is what mothers teach children which is why we love them.

I waited for you. I wanted to find someone who would do things for me and tell me to love her. I waited a long time. When I saw you I thought I had found that 'someone'.

I saw you at a market stall. You were standing with your mother carrying a bag of vegetables. It looked heavy. You must have been eight years old. I wanted to offer to help you. I wanted to ask you whether you would love me. I asked my mother whether I could help you and my mother said 'No'. She said you weren't the one I was waiting for. I was sad and angry at the same time as children can be because I thought you were the one. My mother laughed when I told her I was sure you were the one. She told me that the girl for me would be a princess. As we walked away you didn't look like a princess any more.

The mist lingered longer than it should have. The story stopped for a moment while you took some photographs. You took some photographs of me too. You asked me to move so that you could see the inscription on the headstone. As I was about to move I saw some nettles. I knew if I brushed against them they would sting me. I brushed against them. The pain was mild, not enough. I tore off a clump of nettles ripping my hands as I did so and rubbed

43

them on my face. I was right. Now it hurt me as much as it should. It felt good. The pain made me feel alive. I watched you take photographs wondering who would buy them. I imagined them in a Sunday supplement. I imagined what they'd be like. I imagined comfortable people in comfortable homes commenting on them. I heard them say how sad and beautiful the pictures were.

When you came to our house, I knew my mother was right. It was worth waiting for a princess. You were eleven by then. I loved you completely. Your hair was shoulder length, and your dress above your knees. You wore white socks and stuck your feet in my face. You asked me to smell them. I called you disgusting and pushed them away. You fell on your back and I jumped on top of you and pinned your arms down with my knees. You screamed that I was hurting you. I laughed. I pinched your nose, and then, you started to cry. I let you go, calling you a baby as I did so. You said you hated me. That hurt. You told my mother and she told me off. I wanted to cry. I didn't because I wanted to show you that I was a man. I was strong and could look after you. My mother told me to say 'sorry'. I said 'sorry'. I said I didn't want to hurt you. I said I was only playing. I couldn't hold back the tears any longer. I cried. I said I loved you. You laughed at me and called me a big sissy. Our mothers laughed. I called you a bitch. I had heard my father use that word. My mother slapped me for cursing. I said I hated you, but I didn't really. I wanted to love you forever but you weren't ready. I thought about you for a long time after that. Our parents stopped meeting. I asked my mother why we didn't meet anymore. Our fathers had quarrelled. My mother knew why I asked and told me again that you were not the one. I would have to wait. I had to grow up even more. I had to become as tall as my Dad before I would find you.

I was thirsty. The wine was all gone. You had some water and offered me some. I drank from the bottle that you gave me. I didn't wipe it before I drank as you had done because you were my friend. It was my offer of friendship. You didn't notice. You checked the photographs you had taken. You seemed pleased with them. You looked around to see whether any other memories wanted to be captured. I waited patiently. I wanted to hear the story, the story that you wanted to tell me. You got up and walked away. You left the empty bottle of wine for me. I fell asleep waiting.

I awoke because I was hungry. You weren't there. I looked around to see what I could eat. My head hurt and my throat was dry. The sun hid behind the clouds. The earth still felt cold. My face was sore. I remembered the nettles. I left the head stone that had given me a place to rest. I don't remember who was buried there but thanked him just the same. I assumed it was a man.

I walked along the path, barely visible through the grass and weeds, broken by time. I walked past a tree that had been planted many years ago to breathe life for the spirits not at rest, wandering aimlessly, waiting for something to happen. The trial of life continued through the barrier of physical death, still hoping for something more than mere existence. Self indulgent, self absorbed and forever the beggar waiting for fortune to be kind to him for having patience. I saw you underneath that tree. Your eyes were bloodshot. You must have been crying. You noticed me walk up to you. You affected a smile. I sat down beside you and looked out at the cemetery. You rolled a joint, lit it and disappeared. You continued your story. I couldn't see you, but I could just hear your quiet voice.

I was nineteen when I saw you again. You were at university. You were happy with your friends. I liked the way you brushed your hair into a pony tail, and those strands that you carefully placed behind your ears. You were fresh, captivating, like the first breeze of spring. I wasn't the only one of course. There were lots of vultures after what they could find; spoils of youth that would be left for the old to drool over. I saw you then. I followed you to your halls and sat outside in the park until it was dark. I found out where your rooms were and took comfort in the light that shone for me late into the night. You were studying. I studied too. I studied in the grounds beneath your room. I told the security guard I was waiting for you. I said you had agreed to meet me. He didn't believe me so I left. I found a bus stop on the other side of the road, outside the walls from where I could see your room. No-one suspected. Not until that innocent banter in the refectory with my friends. We argued about who was the most beautiful girl in the university. They didn't understand what love was. It was the time of life when dreams were

46

made to last a night or two, no longer. I saw the group of girls that did the rounds to satisfy their lust and I was glad that you weren't one of them. When my friends asked me, I told them about you. I'm sorry, but I had to tell someone and someone told you. You told me to leave you alone. I saw you with one of the boys. He became your boyfriend, lover and then you got engaged. It was only then that I understood you were not the one. I was sad again. I cried, but not for long, because I knew that you weren't the one.

It was getting dark. The air was still. The cold seeped through my shoes, my clothes still damp.

Whenever I lost hope of seeing you again, you crept into my heart, quiet as death. I was always taken by surprise, pleasant surprise. You said you were my princess and I believed you. I made excuses for your disappearances or your coldness when you didn't feel like returning my love. It didn't matter so long as we were together. We played games that children play. We tested how far we could hurt each other, waiting for one to cry before the other would stop.

I was hungry. I asked the photographer whether he had something to eat. He passed me some bread. I thanked him. I ate the bread, swallowed it with some water, and said a prayer.

We stopped hurting each other after a while. We got bored. We stuck to the routine a good marriage brings which helped us keep out of each other's way. I realised you were not my princess. I realised that you had lied and blamed myself for having believed you. But it was alright because I had nothing better to do. And then, one day, without any warning, you left me.

I picked up a pebble from the many smooth pebbles spat out by the sea that now decorate graves. I saw the silhouette of the empty wine bottle. I aimed before throwing it at the bottle. It knocked the bottle over and the neck snapped off. I smiled. You stopped talking. The story had ended. You picked up the broken neck of the bottle and examined it with the attention of a child. Then, with the jagged neck of the bottle, you slit your wrists.

I smiled. You smiled too. It seems we all like pain.

*   *   *

Kyle

Everything ends with incrimination. Sometimes it is you that are to blame and sometimes, if you're lucky, someone else.

Kyle was an acquaintance I'd known for a long time before we called ourselves friends. We met up once in a while. He was a good laugh, a gentle soul who wouldn't hurt a fly. He really wouldn't, though he definitely wasn't a wimp. He had been unlucky in relationships, usually, I suspect, because he always met girls looking for a guy who was assertive, and he wasn't. He didn't know how. I had known many girls who on a description of Kyle would melt and it always surprised me that when, by chance, one of them would meet him they never hit it off. He seemed pre-destined to have girlfriends who would treat him like shit, leaving him to suffer the pain of the break-up.

I was having a drink with Amy, an ex-girlfriend of mine. She needed advice on a project she was working on when I got a call from Kyle who asked whether I had time to meet up.

Amy became my friend once she realised that it was a mistake to consider our relationship more than a temporary fling. We met up occasionally, either when she was in between relationships or struggling through the last gasps of one that was about to end. I was happy we were friends because she was one of those 'good people' that one occasionally comes across, someone who genuinely cares without expecting more than the pleasure of giving. I'm over simplifying only to avoid getting into an analysis that isn't relevant to the story.

We were about finished when Kyle rang. It was still early, only eight, so I asked Kyle to come over. I hadn't expected Amy to stay on. I told her I would stay at the bar because a friend was coming over. She asked whether she could stay and I wasn't really in a position to refuse.

I was glad she stayed because by the time Kyle arrived it was almost nine-thirty and, for a Wednesday night, it was already getting late. I hadn't banked on him taking an hour and a half to turn up. I introduced them and we sat down for another drink even though we probably had enough to drink already.

We stayed for another hour and left together, going our separate ways. I had a nice time and was pleased that Amy was happy with the input I had given on the project. She said she'd enjoyed the rest of the evening too. It always felt good to see her having a nice time.

♩♩

I met up with Kyle ten days later at a local wine bar. Kyle wasn't happy about a venue that didn't serve beer. After an exchange which remained strained there was a silence. Kyle, not being someone who had moments when he had nothing to say, worried me.

'Are you OK?'
'Yes.'

'You sure Kyle, you look really strange.'

'Stuart, I've got something to tell you... I've seen Amy.'

'That's great, when?'

'Actually, a few days ago.'

'Why didn't you tell me earlier?'

'Well, I knew she was your ex and she told me not to say anything.'

'What? Why?'

'I don't know. She just told me not to say anything.'

'Then, why are you telling me now?' I asked a little irritated.

'Stuart, please...'

'I really don't mind,' I interrupted, 'If you guys hit it off then good luck to you. I told you at the time that it was all over between us, and it is! Amy's a great girl but just not my type, that's all. We're just good friends.'

Kyle fell silent again.

'Look Kyle,' I continued, 'I only went out with her for about a month and the break-up was no great tragedy. We just accepted it as one of those things. Amy's fine about this and I am too.'

Kyle looked pained as if there was something that he wanted to say but was having difficulty putting it into words. I realised that I was being a little insensitive. Calming myself I allowed him time to speak.

'I'm not going out with Amy. She isn't my girlfriend or anything like that, Stuart.'

His reply irritated me.

'Kyle, don't you understand, I don't care! Amy's just a friend.'

'Stuart, wait a minute, that's not what I want to talk about. I mean, not directly anyway.'

I didn't understand what was going on, but apologised anyway and waited for Kyle to speak. This is what he told me.

'Do you remember when we sitting in the bar, you left to go to the loo? Well, I don't know what got into me. I asked Amy whether she'd like to meet up some time. Well, she said 'yes' and gave me her phone number. She told me not to tell you because we'd only just met and she wanted to explain things to you, separately. I agreed, although you have to believe me Stuart, as soon as I had, I felt awful. You're my friend and I felt I was betraying you. It didn't seem right. I wasn't sure whether the two of you had in fact broken up. I know you told me that you had, but Stuart, the fact is that you got on so well together, met so often, always talked about her... all that confused me.'

I listened not sure whether I should be amused or annoyed with the exaggerated difficulties Kyle seemed to have gone through. I settled on the former and smiled.

'Stuart, I mean it, this is serious. You don't understand. I liked Amy and I thought she liked me too.'

I didn't hear him using the past tense at the time.

'So what's the problem? I told you that Amy and I are finished, if in fact something ever began. She's a great girl, and I hope the two of you will be happy together.'

'Stuart! Listen! It's not like that.'

His pained expression returned. He wanted to speak.

'OK Kyle. For God's sake go ahead. I mean, I'm sorry.'

He looked at me for a moment as if to determine whether I was being sincere in my apology and having decided I was, continued.

'Well, I debated whether I should ring her or whether I should speak to you first. I really did. I worried about it for most of the week. I decided to ring her and, if we planned to go out, told myself I would ring you.

Amy wasn't happy when I called her. She was annoyed because I had taken so long to get back to her. She said, I was arrogant for taking so long to call her and, asked me whether I really wanted to see her. I told her I did, and explained that I had only taken so long to get back to her because it worried me that she had asked me not to mention anything to you. She seemed appeased, agreed to meet, said she was glad I'd kept my promise of not telling you and said she would explain when we met up.

We agreed to meet up last Saturday night. I asked her where. She suggested we meet in Soho at a Chinese restaurant she liked. You know how much I hate Chinese food but I didn't say anything. After the way the phone call had begun she didn't give me much of a chance anyway.'

It didn't sound like the Amy I knew, but then again, I think we become different people depending on the person we're with. I remembered the Chinese restaurant. We met there on our first date too. Kyle paused as if to gather his thoughts before continuing. I waited.

'She asked me whether I knew where it was and, as I didn't, we agreed to meet outside

53

the Empire, Leicester Square, and walk up from there.

'I got there early and waited outside the cinema watching the tourists go by. By seven-thirty, Leicester Square was filling up with the influx of cinema goers. Amy appeared about twenty minutes late, but in a great mood. She was happy and we met as if we'd been friends for a long time. She took my arm as we walked past the strip bars and sex shops to the restaurant. She knew where we were going and talked all the way there. She had made a reservation which impressed me.

'We had a wonderful meal and, by the end of it, I was having a great time. I'm sorry Stuart, but to be honest, by the time we finished dinner I had forgotten all about you and Amy. I only remembered later that she'd promised to explain why she had told me not to tell you about our date.'

I prepared myself for what was coming next. It seemed clear to me from the way Kyle was telling me the story that he had taken Amy home and slept with her. He paused for a long time before continuing as if he was allowing me time to think of something to say when he would finally tell me.

It's true Amy and I had slept together a few times but I didn't recall any of them as being memorable. Kyle's lead up to it suggested it must have been memorable for them and, I felt a pang of jealousy, a reaction which surprised me. I checked myself.

'That's fine. Look,' I said, 'I don't mind one bit.'

'I know Stuart. I sort of knew you wouldn't, even though I would have preferred to tell you up front. But that's not the whole of it.'

I stared at him trying to understand what he was leading up to. What had started with boredom, listening to Kyle hooking up with Amy and then, irritation because I thought Kyle expected some reaction at their having slept together, now turned into confusion as I went through all the possibilities of why he'd asked to see me? I waited for Kyle to speak.

'It was late when we finished dinner. You know how dangerous it is on the tube at that time of the night. Anyway, I said I'd take her home and she was happy with that.

'Amy didn't say anything all the way to her place. When we got there, she asked whether I wanted to come in. I said it was getting late and she said I should phone for a minicab. It sounds like a soap opera telling you about what happened but that's the way it was. I hadn't planned to do anything. I know you won't believe me but it's the truth. It's not that I didn't find her attractive, but if this was going to be the start of something, I wanted to wait...didn't want it to start it off like a one night stand.

'When I went in Amy asked whether I wanted a coffee before calling the minicab and I said yes. The meal had been great fun but the journey home was strained. I explained it to myself that maybe Amy thought I was being presumptuous taking her home. I didn't mean anything by it Stuart, I swear! The sentiment was genuine. I genuinely thought it was dangerous for a girl at that time of the night to go home alone.'

He paused again. I was getting worried that Kyle may go into more detail about the seduction that I would feel comfortable listening to. I couldn't understand why I should, but it worried me all the same.

'Amy brought in the coffee and one thing led to another and, well, we ended up in bed.'

That was when I thought 'enough!' I didn't want to hear anymore.

'OK, Kyle I think that's enough. You can spare me the pornographic details. I'm not interested!'

'No, Stuart. It's after that. I don't know what happened, but Amy started to cry. The more I asked her what the matter was, the more inconsolable she became. I didn't know what to do. I tried to comfort her but she pushed me away, screaming at me to leave her alone. I was worried about the neighbours. I didn't really know her, this was a first date and I was in her flat. Suppose, hearing the screams, the neighbours called the police? What would I say? You do understand don't you? I had no choice. It wasn't as if I'd raped her! Stuart, honestly, I had no choice!'

Kyle was crying. No sound, but he actually had tears in his eyes as he spoke. It was seeing his tears that gave me start. I felt as if I had missed something he had told me, some salient fact that would help me piece everything together. There were too many questions that appeared all at once. Why was Amy crying? What was he talking about? What did he mean? Why was he crying?

All sorts of thoughts went through my head. I thought of violence or rape, but Kyle wasn't the type. He was a big sissy.

'Kyle!' I shouted louder than I intended. I noticed a few people at neighbouring tables turn to see what was happening.

He looked up at me. 'I'm sorry'.

'Kyle, will you just stop it. Just tell me what happened!' I said, lowering my voice to a whisper.

I was on tenterhooks. As he tried to speak to me he started crying for real. Not just tears. He was actually crying. He threw his head into his hands unable to control himself. We were by this time definitely making a spectacle of ourselves.

'Kyle, will you get a grip on yourself. You are embarrassing me and yourself!'

'Oh Stuart, I don't know what got into me. She just wouldn't stop screaming. I dragged her out of bed and started hitting her. I was so angry. I don't know why. All I could hear was her screaming. All I wanted was for her to stop. She was frightened. I've never seen fear in a face like that before. She broke away from me and huddled in a corner with her arms trying to protect her face. I was kicking her and shouting at her to stop. She stuffed her hands into her mouth to stop the sounds. She wasn't screaming anymore...just muffled sobs. By the time I came to I was exhausted. I put on my clothes and left.'

I was speechless. I wasn't sure what sort of reaction he expected of me. I wanted to say something, but couldn't find the words. I was angry. I wanted to hit him. I wanted to ask him why he did it. I wanted to understand what had happened, but all I felt was disgust. I thought of Amy and what she'd been through. I wanted to call the police, have him arrested, shout at him, but in my rage, unable to do anything, I grabbed my jacket and left.

When I got home I rang Amy. There was no answer. It was late, but I needed to speak to her. I got in my car and drove to her place. I rang her door bell for what seemed like ages and she finally opened the door. She was in a dressing gown. As soon as she saw me she flung herself sobbing into my arms.

I wanted to ask her what had happened, but she was so distraught I didn't press her. She looked awful. The bruises on her face, arms and legs looked as if she'd been in an accident. I didn't know what to do other than hold her as she cried herself to sleep.

I didn't sleep that night. Amy slept soundly on my lap. Dawn was breaking when Amy got up to go to the bathroom. I was still sitting on the sofa when she got back. She didn't switch on the light.

'I'm going to bed.' she said. 'You can leave when you want to.'

She turned and left. I heard her close the bedroom door, sat on the sofa for a few minutes, and then got up and left too.

♫♫♫

I never found out what happened that night, and never saw Kyle again. He rang me a few times, but I had absolutely no interest in speaking to him. I haven't spoken to Amy either.

58

I haven't called and neither has she. This is an episode of my life that I want to forget, but after all this time, it still haunts me. As I said, everything ends with incrimination. Sometimes it is you that are to blame and sometimes, if you're lucky, someone else.

*   *   *

Sally

J

It wasn't long before things got bad enough for Sally to realise what she had gotten herself in to. As if the routine was not enough, the little arguments that arise out of the most absurd of situations began to grate. If it wasn't forgetting to buy something, it was warming up last night's dinner and serving it up because there wasn't the desire to cook. These things had happened before but it seemed that of late everything was a cause of irritation. Sally put it down to difficulties at work that Chris wouldn't talk about. The thought that Chris might lose his job did cross her mind but that was unlikely since it had only been a few months since, following a glowing recommendation, Chris had been promoted. It was on the day of the celebration for the promotion, and the love making that followed, that Chris had asked her to move in with him and she had agreed. She had been expecting the invitation for some weeks so that when the time came she took Chris by surprise when she immediately agreed.

Sally enjoyed playing the role of the housewife. The fact that she worked and wasn't married didn't matter. She began to rearrange things around the flat to make it more like home almost immediately. She had asked Chris whether he minded her making a few changes. He said he didn't so she made them. That changed when on the day she moved a picture, the only one in the sitting room when they had their first scene. He reminded her that he hadn't agreed she could do anything she wanted and, for good measure, threw in that he was sick to death of coming home every evening to find something else had changed. When she protested he reminded her that it was his flat.

Sally was hurt. She had nowhere to go. Her flat was let. She had wanted to let it for six months but Chris had said that as she'd found a good tenant she might as well let it for a year. There were seven months to go. It wasn't the thought of being homeless that hurt; it was more personal than that. However the fact that she didn't have anywhere to go meant she could stay for as long as she wanted and he couldn't do anything about it made it bearable. Chris could be mean but he wouldn't throw her out. Chris was angry. He had a shower, changed his clothes and went out without saying goodbye.

Sally had a little cry to relieve the tension and fell asleep.

Chris came back late with the smell of beer. He said he was sorry. Sally knew he would be. He explained that he had a bad day at work and it was his favourite painting. She apologised, they kissed, she knew what he wanted and, although she wasn't in the mood, gave in. He came before his drunken clumsiness became uncomfortable for which she was grateful. She moved the painting back the next day. Where the picture hung wasn't important. When Chris came home that evening he moved it back to where Sally had moved it in the first place saying, with an air of magnanimity, that he loved her more than the picture and she could put it

61

wherever she wanted. Sally said she loved him too, and meant it.

Sally always discussed her relationships with Anne, her best friend at work. She told her what had happened the previous evening, including the love making, and Anne, based on the experience of marriage of thirteen years, told her she had nothing to worry about as that was normal. She said that Sally was merely entering the world of domesticity which required her to remember the good times when things were bad.

Sally knew about the good times. She liked having someone to look after and the thought that she had someone to look after her was a plus. She liked the idea of coming home to a flat that wasn't empty. The fact she wouldn't have to risk the disappointment, or worse, of one-night stands or the humiliation of accepting invitations from old boyfriends in between relationships when there was no one else. She was free to go out whenever she wanted to but didn't always like the idea of having to pay what seemed to be the inevitable cost of being entertained. That was good. She didn't have to cope with having to feel like a slut just because she occasionally felt like escaping the loneliness of being a single girl just the wrong side of thirty. She'd thought about getting a dog but, when Chris came along, she decided that he was a lot better, most of the time.

Chris, on the other hand was more accepting of the circumstances in which he found himself and their whirlwind romance, if it was that. He hadn't played the romantic before and thought it would make a nice change. If he was honest, he didn't expect it to come with the baggage of domesticity. He wasn't complaining. It had its upside.

Sally was a perfect choice. Her reputation was intact. She had just come through an unpleasant relationship and wasn't ready for another one just yet. Chris read that reluctance as being the mark of a girl who didn't sleep around; too old to be a virgin but a good subject for the experiment. He was good with women and lately had been a little too successful. Having whoever might be available was getting boring. When he asked Sally whether he could call her, the fact that she said 'no' was a welcome change. Sally gave no excuses. It was the initial 'no' that started it all.

Sally was wary of the flowers at first, but soon began to enjoy being the talk of the office. After the third bouquet delivered to the office she began to waver, now more from embarrassment that excitement; she felt she had to give something in return. It was the tickets to see a show that gave her the opportunity.

Chris did very well. He planned buying flowers on the spur of the moment and, never forgot to buy little inexpensive presents, tokens he called them, to surprise her. He practiced the terms of endearment which he recited with the same trite alacrity that actors in black and white movies had been successful with. He was surprised at the ease at which she believed everything he said or did which he attributed to evidence of her wholesome goodness for which he complimented himself for having found. He played the game for about two months. Sally gave in, the conquest complete. A successful close of a deal negotiated with the ease of financial genius that comes with good planning. Once he knew he'd won, he waited for her to see through it.

It was waiting for Sally to see through it that was the mistake. He didn't mean to ask Sally to move in with him. In fact, that was the first time her innocence irritated him. He hadn't thought the part he played could be taken that seriously. After all it was the first time he had asked her. Any sensible girl would have said 'no' or said that it was too soon. He would then at least have had a breather and, either escape with relief or, accept that it might be time for him to settle down. He thought any fool would have to come to realise it was just an experiment. But once Sally had said 'yes', she was so excited. She told him she'd expected the invitation and could move in at the weekend. Even when he had regained his composure and tried to get out of it with the excuse of having to go out of town on business that weekend which he thought would give him some respite, Sally, instead of taking the hint, replied that it couldn't have been planned any better. She could move in and wait for him when he got back.

Chris felt like an idiot turning up to see a brother he hadn't telephoned for over a year, and hadn't seen for three, asking whether he could stay the weekend. His brother was speechless, but it all worked out in the end.

♩♩

That was a few months ago and Chris was getting used to the idea of having Sally around. He didn't much enjoy the arguments but liked the idea of getting away with them; knowing he could have a row that wouldn't end in Sally leaving him.

Sally was getting used to it too. Although she knew he occasionally had bad moods, a change in life style meant she didn't notice when the incidence of moodiness increased. Sometimes she would sulk and, sometimes she would let him know he had gone too far. More often than not they would end up making love, which didn't always end up being a chore.

♩♩♩

The neighbour's cat died. Sally spent dinner telling Chris how it upset the old lady in the flat across the hallway. It was strange but did he know how people got rid of a dead cat? At that point Chris asked her to stop, she was making him feel sick, asked her to change the subject and pass the ketchup. The silence that followed was broken when Chris unexpectedly asked her whether she fancied seeing a film the next day. She replied she would love to. It was gossiping with Anne at work the next morning that Sally realised she hadn't even asked him which one.

'I don't know, Anne, but we are going out. It doesn't really matter; they're all the same anyway.'

Anne thought she was silly but hoped she'd have a great time. She did. It made a change. Sally didn't have many friends and she was happy that she didn't need any. She'd had enough of trying to make friends that would last.

She had been through three that she classified as serious relationships, the last of which ran on for almost two years.

$$\mathcal{JV}$$

The affairs were many though rarely memorable, but that was all in the past. This was her new life now. Walking arm in arm with someone she loved and knowing 'home' meant the same for both of them.

On Saturdays, when Chris went out on some errand or other, she would sit by the window with a cup of tea and think of them.

Gerry was the one she remembered most. He was the one she'd felt sure would be with her forever. Jim was the one who had promised to be the one. By the time she told him he was her first it was too late. He had gone too far to stop. She learned to cry after Jim. She didn't meet anyone for almost a year after that. When she did it was an indifferent one-night stand. She called herself a slut for sleeping with him, whatever his name was, which made her feel better. It became easier after that. A series of one night stands followed.

Men, she decided, couldn't be figured out. Their games were tiresome and, the ones that promised the most came too soon. The boredom was only to be expected. Gerry was the one she wanted. He was fun. Not much good in bed but the foreplay was great. When he left her it wasn't melodramatic. No excuses. He just didn't call her and when she called him he was always busy. She had to be told.

'Take a hint, sweetheart. It was good while it lasted. Don't spoil it.'

Sally didn't, although, she hoped he'd burn in hell.

The married ones were always more attentive. They flirted as if the safety of marriage gave them the right to play the game. Marriage was their safety net when they tired of playing around. Sally had seen it so many times at work. When she worked as a relief secretary, she saw more than most.

Chris always came back tired on those Saturday jaunts with excuses for being late; the garage had ripped him off, the traffic was awful or, simply complaining at having to work at weekends. Sally had got used to the routine. After the excuses they always went out for a drink in the evening or met friends for a meal and Chris was particularly nice. Sally liked those evenings. There was always a lot of laughter, the company was always good and she enjoyed being a part of it.

Chris had been gone a long time. The brakes had been playing up and Chris said that a friend of his had a mate who had promised to take a look at the car. Sally was a little disappointed because he hadn't mentioned it the night before, but she was happy he promised to come back soon. He was a kind man. He even gave her a hug and a kiss before he left which wasn't always the case. She washed up, made herself a cup of tea and smelled her hair trying to identify the smell Chris said turned him on. He had his tender moments and they were worth waiting for.

Someone else had said he liked the smell of her hair. It was Hugh. He was married.

Sally met Hugh when his secretary was off on maternity leave. He was a serious man who worked hard and stayed late in the office. He had two children, a son eleven and a daughter who was seven. His wife, a plain looking woman sat on his desk in a black and white studio photograph and hardly ever rang him at the office. The other secretaries said he was hard to work for but Sally, more accepting than most, didn't. She often stayed late especially when she had nothing to do. She didn't mind. Hugh was always politely grateful.

'I'm off.'

'Thanks Sally. Have a nice weekend.'

'Are you alright?'

Hugh was sitting in his office with his feet on the desk having a cigarette. It was nearly eight and he didn't look as if he was ready to go home.

'Why don't you go home,' said Sally. 'We've finished the report and the slides are ready for your presentation on Monday.'

'I will in a minute, you go ahead.'

Sally said goodnight and left.

The station was packed. There had been a derailment and trains were being cancelled.

Sally had 40 minutes before the next train and there wasn't much else to do except wait. She remembered it was the weekend and she hadn't made any plans. She would do some washing and some shopping on Saturday but that left Sunday free.

'Hello Sally, you still here?'

He made her jump.

'Sorry, didn't mean to startle you.'

'No, that's alright, I was miles away.'

'How long have you got?

'About half an hour.'

'Fancy coming over for a drink?'

They were all the same really, merely variations on the theme.

Hugh lived in a large detached house, with a drive, out in the country. The car, a jaguar parked at the station car park, was used to waiting. There wasn't anyone at the station. It was one of those where no station staff worked after eight in the evening.

Few passengers got off the train and it was a dark drive to the house. Hugh didn't say very much on the drive home. Sally wondered whether Hugh realised how lucky he was. She wondered whether he would be gentle. He seemed the sort who would be.

He made some pasta while Sally took a shower. The pink bathrobe smelled of his wife so she took his. She came downstairs to the smell of food. She was hungry. She sat on a barstool while he finished off cooking the meal. She smiled as he placed two plates, each with a clean embroidered napkin.

He seemed very much at ease. He asked her whether she preferred red or white and opened the bottle of wine without much effort. They ate the meal with a restraint that anticipated what was to follow. The conversation was polite, the compliments sweet, and she marvelled at the way he ate with the grace that comes of good living. The food was good, fresh, and the wine heady.

He was gentle and unhurried. He played the part as someone who had done this before and knew the rules. Sally fell asleep thankful it wasn't as bad as it could have been. She knew how bad it could be. The bruises picked up from a drunk who had virtually raped her for one.

In the morning Hugh had made breakfast before she awoke.

'The bathrobe suits you. I think you should have it,' he said with a smile.

'Thanks, I think I will.' Sally didn't feel a like a slut. She was comfortable. She knew it wasn't going to last. She had known that the moment she'd agreed to go home with him. Sunday was taken care of.

It was a sunny Saturday morning much like this one except the French windows that looked out on a garden proudly boasted that no amateur gardeners had a hand in the way it looked. The view from the flat was hardly that, but there was a nice garden and the trees were full of summer after a night of rain.

Sally still had the bathrobe. It wasn't a painful memory because it had no lies or false hope. No promises that would be forgotten in the hum drum routine that familiarity always brought. She didn't feel sorry for his wife because she knew she wasn't the first and, she reasoned, if it hadn't been her it would have been someone else. The logic worked for her. The bathrobe still smelled of that weekend.

Chris often joked about her buying a man's bathrobe and she laughed with him. She didn't let on. There was no need, and anyway, he wouldn't understand. She often wondered how Hugh explained the missing bathrobe to his wife, but she never discussed his wife with him. Neither did Hugh.

ᘖᘒ

She saw Chris drive into the road. He looked good in casuals. The way he slammed the car door shut showed he was pleased with himself. She loved him. It was moments like this that made the arguments irrelevant, no matter how frequent she knew they would eventually become. She was glad she didn't have to go out looking for someone. She could wait for Chris at home. Knowing he would always come home was enough. She couldn't be happier.

*   *   *

Boiling eggs

J

You know they say it takes three minutes to boil an egg. Well, it doesn't. It takes forever. First you have to wait for the water to boil, then, once the water's boiled, you have to wait 5 minutes, sometimes more, sometimes less. There's a question whether you place the eggs in cold water or, whether you wait until the water has already started to boil before dropping in the God damned eggs! The real question is however, 'who gives a shit!'

And then, when you think they're ready, you place the eggs under a cold tap to cool them down before you start to peel off the eggshell. That's when the fun starts. You're peeling those eggs over the bin (so you don't have to clear up afterwards) and what happens? You burn your fingers! The bloody eggs are still damned hot under the eggshell.

Don't get me wrong! I'm not one of those miserable bastards, moaning about everything (although I've often thought I should become one and join the rest of the human race) it's just that I'm sick to death about having to make the effort!

Living on your own is meant to be fun. Free as a bird and all that. I tell you its shit! You never have anyone when you want them, and when you've finally given up caring a damn, someone offers you a dozen roses. By the way, I am speaking metaphorically. I'm not like that! All the other times you spend either getting drunk, nursing a hangover or out with friends as desperate as you are, slagging off girls, rubbishing football managers or players or, boasting about exploits that you have to be drunk to believe.

I met her last summer. She was cute. I fantasised, you know, the beginning of a lifelong friendship and all that, but she wasn't interested. I even changed my looks, brushing my hair the wrong way, and my style, to see whether I could interest her in something, but being the stupid cow she is, she didn't like 'cool' (the hair gel obviously didn't work). I tried sophisticated but she didn't bite. Maybe the tweed jacket that I bought second hand to for the worn look (and save some money) didn't go with the jeans I was wearing or, maybe it was the brown shoes that I thought were all the rage. Hell, I even tried the anxious teenager 'I don't know what I want but maybe that's love' approach. No, she was good. She led me on for three dates before becoming busy.

It's a strange sensation to burn your fingers when you don't have to. I mean, I could have left them for a while, the eggs, remember them, but sometimes just for the sheer hell of it, you sort of want to feel alive and that's what I was doing with those eggs, burning my bloody fingers.

I couldn't decide what to have them with toast or cold bread out of the fridge. Yeah, I know, you're asking why I put bread in the fridge. If you ask the question then you're not on your own. You wouldn't know that bread lasts longer in the fridge. When they start making half loaves (for half the price) I'll buy a bread bin.

Anyway, to hell with the eggs! I decided to have them with bread; two sandwiches and, while I was carefully holding one of them, the phone rang.

Ok, now you get the picture, don't you? I'm holding the sandwich carefully to make sure egg doesn't fall out and make a mess that yours truly will have to clear up. I know I could use a plate but then who the hell is going to wash it afterwards? So I'm carefully holding this sandwich with both hands and then, half way through the sandwich, the telephone rings.

'Hi, it's me.'

Who the hell is 'me'? I'm racking my brain to figure out who it is. You know, going through all the people that could be ringing me. The fact it's a girl should make it easier, but it doesn't.

'Hi.'

'It's been a while.'

Silence while the penny drops!

'I haven't heard from you for a long time. How are you?' she continues.

My sandwich is now on the work top, the boiled egg scattered all around me and she asks me how I am! Gimme a break! And anyway, she's the one that stopped returning my calls so what the hell does she want now. It's been three months at least! But I'm polite, even though it's bloody rich that she doesn't even give me her name. Just expects this lonely bastard to know who she is after three months.

'Hi, yeh, I'm fine. How are you?'

Do I really care as I see what's left of my sandwich on the work top, egg yolk oozing out from in between the two slices of bread already soggy from where I was holding the sandwich?

'I'm fine. What have you been up to?'

Do I tell her I've been boiling eggs! That I am walking around in a t-shirt and boxer shorts, that I don't know why she's calling me when I already don't give a damn. Nah, I don't want the sandwich any more. It looks disgusting!

She called me up once before. She had a row with her boyfriend. I thought my luck was in but she chickened out at the last moment. Well, it was OK because I didn't have any 'you-know-whats'. And besides, I didn't have anywhere to go. My flatmate was in, horny ogling bastard that he is, not to mention being a tight fisted prat who always owes me rent and never tidies up.

'Nothing much.'

'Just rang, thought we could meet up? Catch a (soppy) film.'

The tips of my fingers are tingling. Those eggs were hot. I'm sure I've burned them. My fingers, I mean.

♪♪

It *was* a soppy film. I got bored after just five minutes. It was obvious what was going to happen, and yet I had to wait for the stupid script writer to take his pound of flesh with no bloody lawyers to help me out. Ninety-one minutes without an intermission. I checked.

They don't do intermissions anymore because they need to get in as many shows as they can. They've got thirteen screens and one person in each of them with the cushy job of pressing the play button. It's only DVDs I'm sure. Thirteen boiling halls with no air-conditioning and some idiot with a huge bag of popcorn that a cow would be happy to chew for the rest of her life, or at least until the farmer sends her to get electrocuted and pack a million packs of beef slices that feed the lonely. Or idiots with gallon size paper cups; recyclable of course cause you don't want those 'greens' coming and trashing the place in protest, that sit behind you making disgusting slurping sounds that probably belong in a porn show!

She looked in my direction a few times and I smiled as sincerely as you would. You know, I'm normal. I just don't get it that's all, all that hypocrisy that goes by the label of compatible social behaviour. Smile, look cheerful, be helpful, don't get angry with those that you don't know; all the stuff that you need to do to avoid the men in white coats coming and taking you away.

She squeezed my hand once or twice. I didn't get that either! I never get those stupid gestures that mean exactly the opposite of what you might think. The worst bit is they always get away with it. I mean, when I try and do that luvvy duvvy stuff they look at me as if I'm stoned, and when I don't, I'm told I'm just a cold, heartless uncaring bugger. I mean, it's not as if I just let it come out naturally. I mean, I've checked the luvvy duvvy look. I've practiced it in front of a mirror and while it might look a little weird on me, like in those silent movies, it looks pretty damn strange on girls too.

I remember half way through the film laughing out loud. I really couldn't help it. I mean I just thought the place was so damn boiling and you can guess what I remembered......those eggs. Even after spending like two hundred years under cold water tap they were still boiling under the shell. And, after I had peeled them both I cut the first one open and the yoke spilled out immediately clinging to my fingers like something out of a sci-fi movie. She gave me a strange look. Boy, was I glad we were in a cinema because can you imagine me trying to explain the whole thing to her laughing my head off. Too right, she wouldn't have got it! Yeah, well, I said sorry and started watching the film thinking about how I would explain it afterwards, just in case she remembered to ask.

I was getting real stressed about it I can tell you which is why I let off a silent fart that I had been clenching my cheeks forever

77

trying to hold in. She looked at me as soon as the smell rose to tickle her nose (farts rise, you know) and I whispered in her ear.

'Sorry, that's what I was laughing at. Didn't you hear it?'

'Disgusting!' she said.

I agreed. Ok Watson, I think we are done here. Sherlock Holmes solves another mystery! I think Holmes will have to go easy on the eggs in future! McDonalds after the film!

♪♪♪

OK, I know I said McDonalds, but old Ronald doesn't win all the time. Sometimes, you have to give the coagulating, lukewarm, tasteless Chinese stuff a go.

'I'm not really in the mood for a McDonalds. Do you fancy a Chinese?'

Yeah, take away, sweetheart and you're on.

'No, that's OK. I'm sure there must be one around nearby.'

'I know where there's one.'

Bet you do, giving me the run around. Lucky I went to the money machine before I met her. I took out thirty quid which I hoped would be more than enough. I mean, let's face it; I could pick up a tart for fifty. Maybe not in Mayfair but I'm sure I could somewhere.

The Chinese was exactly as you would imagine it to be; a selection of pre-cooked dishes ordered by the number. She knew the names and in Chinese; obviously trying to impress me but I was playing it cool.

'I'm not a great fan of Chinese but love to try whatever you're having. We can share the dishes.'

That was her cue! I then listened to the lecture she gave the waiter which I'm sure she was making up, but I looked suitably impressed. I mean you must be some sad git to read up on different Chinese food and then talk about it in a restaurant.

'I didn't know you were such an expert.'

'Well,' said the condescending cow, 'you have to know about these things.'

I was tempted to reply but I let it go.

I wanted a lager but, after the lecture, I was worried that I would end up having to listen to another one. I ordered green tea that looked and tasted like the water the eggs had been boiled in, but I didn't let on.

The food came. The plate was chipped. She ate the rice with chop sticks scooping it into her mouth as if she were Chinese. The waitress came over dressed in that fake oriental stuff with the slit on the side that rode up to the tops of stockings that were just visible. She must have been a hundred, with a grin that comes with centuries of affected deference.

'Evlitin aal lite?'

'Yes, thank you,' I smiled, wanting to add, 'I'm just on this penance of a date. Seen a soppy movie and ended up at your place when I could have been having a McRoyal with cheese, fries and a shake at half the

79

price. Something Travolta and that other guy, Jackson would have enjoyed before making the mess they made. I'll send them over later if you like.'

You know what gets me every time? It's the cliché that life really is. I'm not saying that watching eggs boil is better, but God! Doesn't anything ever change? Here am I, sitting with this really cute girl who I don't want any more but loved to have had three months ago. You always get offered what you want when you don't want it anymore!

The bill came and she offered to go 'Dutch'. Yeh, well gimme a break! As if that was real. I mean, I know I'm tight but I don't let a girl pay, not even if she's the one sitting across this greasy table.

'No, don't be silly, my treat.'

Phew, that was close, a fiver left over.

The soppy movie and the Chinese encouraged her to take my arm as we walked out of the restaurant which made me feel good.

OK, now my brain started working. Play too hard and get nothing. Play too soft and, well, get nothing. Tried sophistication, coolness, laid back, jack the lad and all the rest. Nah, it was too much like hard work. I wasn't going to go through all that again and get disappointed. Better to try nothing and then well, at least I could lie to myself that I didn't want it anyway.

'I suppose it's getting late?'

It was nearly eleven and you know what happens to Cinderella at midnight, shoe or no shoe.

'That was a really nice evening. I really enjoyed it.' she nuzzled, laying her head on my shoulder. There was just a moment when I thought.... but no, I wasn't going to make a fool of myself again. After all, remember what I had been through. I wasn't going to misread a hint that wasn't intended.

'So, you taking me home?'

'Yeh, sure. It's late and you know what crap you find on the tube late at night,' I said.

It was just my luck not to find any crap, not even a drunk to protect her from. I was hoping she didn't notice. She didn't say anything so maybe she didn't.

When we got to her place I was knackered. I forgot she lived all the way up in Acton Town. I was going to have fun getting back to Colliers Wood, all the way south on the Northern Line. It must have been passed midnight. I didn't have a watch. I would probably be night bussing it home.

She didn't say a thing all the way down the road from the tube station. I thought she might let me off the hook even though I could've said half the way down the road, 'Look, you can find your way home now. I've done my bit.' I wanted to but well, if I was going to say that I wouldn't have suffered all the suffering of the evening would I?

It was when we got to her front door that she spoke.

'Why don't you come in for a bit?'

OK, now I am not that stupid! I know there are hints I don't get and others that I imagine, and both make me feel stupid. I had five quid in my pocket and, at this time of the night I was definitely going to find a cash machine, and be stupid enough to use it!

Yeh yeh yeh, I know you are thinking, 'Hasn't this git got a credit card.' Well yes I had one but the stupid bank only gave me credit of two hundred and I have been paying the minimum off for the last two months, and yes I am going to risk a mini-cab driver that's been through it all before turn to me and say, 'Well, Sir, American Express will do nicely. Anything else is crap and unless you show me the money sunshine that's what you want to be turned into!'

So I went in. She made some coffee; we kissed, and went to bed.

♫

You know what it's like waiting for eggs to boil. Remember, I told you. It's like waiting for ever. Remember what it's like burning your fingers, all in the name of having something to eat. Well, that's what it's like; the tingling sensation of half scalded finger tips that reminds you you're alive.

Staring at the ceiling with her arm over my chest, her hair in a mess and playing with her fingers while she slept, I tried to remember all I'd gone through to get here. And, you know, all I could think of, despite all the shit you have to go through, was the pleasure you get when those bloody eggs come out perfect!

*　　*

Jack

The loneliness of this life in the hope that something good is sure to happen if we wait long enough is, I'm sure you will agree, a sad way to live, and yet, that's exactly how so many of us live our lives. For all the slogans that urge us to seize the day, so many of us wait for the good life and, until it comes, infuse the 'waiting time' with routine or habit or, forever trying to convince ourselves that this is as good as it gets...for the time being.

There are some of us who assert our belief in a higher order that encourages us to accept that nothing ever changes. Reincarnation after reincarnation continues the hum drum existence until such imaginary time when, due to an accident which we call divine intervention, we realise nirvana. You have to hope something good will happen even though you know deep down that there are no destinations, just the continuation of the journey. Even the atheist avoids accepting that death is the final destination, seeking redemption in some deviant belief born of scientific credibility.

Jack was a good friend. Applied himself in his work and waited for his personal life to take shape. It was strange to see that he had such resilience as he had a history of attracting relationships doomed to failure.

'The next one will be different!' he always used to say, and then merrily went on his way until he came across exactly the same type of person as he had met previously, claiming at the same time that this time it would be different. It reminds me of the story of Abraham who, deciding that idol worship was a waste of time chose to worship the sun. When the sun set he realised he'd made a mistake and decided to worship the moon, and then sat back confused when day broke. Tradition has it that it was then that he realised that God was not a thing but a presence, unseen, omnipotent and everlasting. Human beings are not. Our reason is clouded with the confusion caused by hope, the confusion of searching for a destination embodied by another human being without realising, as Abraham did, that in the world of the material there is no destination that lasts forever.

'You just wait and see! This time it *will* last forever,' and we humoured him. It bothered me that I couldn't tell him he was making another mistake. I wondered sometimes whether we really were his friends.

I once suggested that one of us should tell him that it really is 'the same shit another day', that nothing ever changes, no decisions are ever final and no relationship ever remains the same as we imagine it. My friends, horrified at my suggestion, accused me of being a miserable bastard for not allowing a friend to enjoy the happiness of delusion. The truth is that I'm not a miserable bastard. It was only a momentary arrogance on my part that I thought the truth would somehow make him happy in the long run. Now, on reflection, I'm glad my friends talked me out of it. Not because I didn't care

84

enough to fight for what I thought was right but because I knew that even if we had told him he wouldn't have believed us. That is the reality of how desperately we need hope to get through life.

It was boring to listen to Jack at the beginning of a relationship. Almost as boring as it was to listen to him moan about it at the end of one. I shouldn't really complain as it gave us something to talk about when he wasn't around.

With the children old enough to have found ways to entertain themselves without us, my wife and I were left with not much else to do, other than enjoy the diversion friends like Jack provided or, mourn the passing of the years in a routine, with 'Friday night lies' that gave us the feeling of being alive rather than just existing.

Jack was ever the optimist, as I've said and, we were the realists wondering what it would have been like to have some of those imagined affairs without getting caught. The thought was not seen as betrayal but rather a desperate attempt to alleviate the monotony of repetition.

In a way it was only the fear caused by the failures of friends around us that kept us going. I know my wife, creeping closer to the age of forty, finds herself in a panic about losing her looks. I know nothing can help her at those moments. I, being a man, thought like one and decided she was afraid that the loss of her looks would cause me to leave her or have an affair that I would have the cruelty to admit to.

The pretence doesn't last forever because it doesn't need to. It passes through the pleasure of hunting and conquests, exaggerated because of their infrequency, on through the pleasure of sex more or less on demand, beyond the pretence that familiarity brings and then, further beyond the disaffection to that sublime state that we often see in our parents; the practical togetherness that old couples need to get through each day. Such rational stoicism doesn't have much place in the reality of relationships.

I loved my wife. I told her so, but now it was without the desperate conviction of earlier years of passion, before the children sapped the energy that we previously saved for each other.

Jack found true love again; Heidi this time. An English girl of English parents who believed they were European and thought to publicise that virtue in the name they gave to their only daughter. A pretty girl that had never married, although she was well versed in relationships that lasted for as long as it took for either the talk of children or marriage to end them.

They met at a party which was no more than a modified singles bar where single people came together to experience the guiltless fishing of catching trout in a trout farm. There was something familiar about the couple they made; both tired of looking, they perceived true love as if they were back at school, with absolutely no idea where any of this was leading to.

It took Jack and Heidi a month before they decided to move in together. Money was not much of a concern as both had manageable mortgages. Jack was happy to let Heidi enjoy her property, for the time being, without the hassle needed to consolidate their assets. I think Heidi liked the idea too.

They were fun loving, enjoyed the parties and shared hangovers together with the consideration one normally reserves for strangers. They laughed a lot and seemed to enjoy once again the juvenile exuberance of getting drunk without the embarrassment of waking up with the regret of what might have been said the night before.

I knew Jessica, my wife, envied her even though she would never admit that to me. That was what marriage was for us; protestations of openness and honesty that time had educated us into being selective about sharing our feelings. It wasn't her fault because we all want to break free, despite the fact that very few of us ever can leave behind the safe environment of marriage for very long. I felt sorry for Jessica when not consumed with self pity. The house, the children, the pleasure of friends with common trials and tribulations, all drove our feelings into those dark recesses that we only opened to strangers.

It went on for about a year. Jack and Heidi fell into a world that became more distant to us. We heard of them more through mutual friends than actually meeting with them. They were wild, exciting, went on holidays that family budgets had long moved beyond our psychological reach and which, more through force of habit rather than fact, were destined to never return.

More attention was given to dresses and hair salon visits as Jessica struggled to convince her reflection in the mirror that she still had what it took. I watched her beauty fade with sadness. The freshness of her skin, the confidence of her figure and her excitement, all waned with the certainty of the years.

I think it was when we heard that Jack and Heidi were talking of getting married that we started taking more of an interest in their relationship. Almost three years had passed in the revelry of the carefree 'thirty something's' and, I suppose we expected the relationship to either end or, take a step towards the permanency of marriages that still smacks of respectability. Marriage is still the noble institution, despite the legacy of the sixties which perhaps men exploited better than women. Marriage survives because many still think of the stigma of illegitimate children or, neither is strong enough to risk a new relationship.

I was surprised when Jessica said that she had spoken to Jack and invited them over for dinner. It was one of those conversations that fell into our dinner when we were alone; the children having gulped the food down with speed to allow them those extra precious minutes to chat to friends or watch television. They were too old to listen to advice about healthy eating or indeed anything for that matter. Advice to them brought accusations of us 'moaning again' and we had become too old to cope with the trauma of a family row at dinner. We realised, after such rows, the children would still succeed in leaving the dining table early while we, nursing our wounds would sleep at either end of the king size bed that had been bought for more engaging escapades.

'That should be fun. When are they coming over?'

'When they get back from holiday. Maldives this time.'

I noticed the slight. I wanted to say to Jessica that we ought to do it one day, but something stopped me. I remembered the number of times I had said that and done nothing about it. I didn't want a repeat of an idle conversation that hurt with envy each time the subject was brought up or, bring up those useless excuses that prevented us doing what we said we should. We both knew the excuses were unnecessary and we only used them to hide the absurdness we felt at having the idea in the first place.

JJ

Jack and Heidi were late. They telephoned to say they were going to be late, not realising that would mean Jessica and I would have nothing to do for the extra hour they'd given us. The television was switched on as usual providing the comfort of background noise. The children were either out or at a sleepover so we sat waiting in silence punctuated with random thoughts that elicited little or no response.

Jessica had been preoccupied of late. Initially I had thought it was the monthly usual, but if it was, they were increasingly lasting for longer periods than I remembered. The day had been spent with both of us very much in our own environment: Jessica in the house pottering around and I, either washing the car or, slumped in front of the television. It was strange not

89

having the children around to provide the distraction we needed to cope with each other.

'What do you think about Jack and Heidi getting married?

'What do you mean?'

'Do you think Jack will make it this time?'

'I don't know.'

The response irritated me. I was making conversation but felt ignored.

'I hope they do. Jack deserves a break from having nothing but disasters.'

Jessica didn't respond and I gave up trying. Times like these came and went, and we carried on much as before.

The hour took a long time to pass. I think we both were relieved when we heard the front door bell. It cheered us both up no end to see Jack and Heidi. I wonder whether they were surprised by how glad we were to see them.

'Sorry about being late. You know what women are like.'

It was a stock answer used more for effect than providing an explanation. The girls ignored us.

We hugged and kissed, took their coats and Jack and I went in to the living room. Jessica and Heidi were still in the hallway chatting away. We sat down making ourselves comfortable when Jessica and Heidi walked in.

'Scott, that's a bit rude,' Jessica interrupted 'aren't you going to get some drinks.'

'Oh, sorry, I thought you were going to be a while,'

I got the drinks and we settled into the explosive chatter of people who meet after an abnormal period of absence and have too much to say. The dinner was good, as it always was, and Jack and I cleared up leaving the girls at the table. They seemed to have a lot to talk about.

It was going to be a church wedding and Heidi was going to be in white. That was expected. The previous weddings had been the same. I suppose the only thing that surprised us was that it was going to be the following summer which seemed a long time to wait, but they explained they didn't want to rush things. They wanted everything to be perfect and Heidi, almost as if to reassure herself, showed us the engagement ring, telling us the long version of how Jack had proposed to her. How romantic everything had been, how much she loved Jack and how wonderful everything was. Based on Jack's reactions I wondered whether he too thought she was trying too hard.

It's nice seeing two people in love. I thought of how much we were in love, Jessica and I, but each time I looked at her I had to chase away doubts that appeared like flies buzzing around me. She was still beautiful and I did love her, but she was not the girl I fell in love with. It was not that she was older. It was just that there always seemed to be something missing. For some reason, through all the years of struggling to balance bringing up children with careers, we had somehow lost the will to remind ourselves why we got married in the first place.

I was glad that I was married to her, glad to have the children we had, even though we seemed to see less of them than we would have liked, glad that we had a reasonably comfortable

91

life that allowed us a decent holiday each year and, glad about all the common friends we had.

There were many things that were good about our marriage, but as time passed, trying to remember the benefits of marriage required more effort. Conversations became either communicating information that was needed such as what time I would be home, would Jessica have time to pick up the car from the garage where it was being serviced or, having an argument that, more often than not, left us unable to remember why the argument had started in the first place. It became rare that we would communicate emotion. The sex was more a result of physical desire than emotional passion. When we had sex it was clear at the outset that is what was needed rather than flowing on from a desire for closeness. When either of us was not in the mood, we would make an effort to oblige the other which resulted in the mechanical exertion that thankfully tired us out enough to fall asleep at the same time rather than irritate each other trying to engage in idle conversation. It was a good marriage and it was satisfying that, despite the protestations of love and romance, Jack and Heidi would also, if they were lucky, enjoy a similar end.

♪♪♪

Jessica left me soon after that day Jack and Heidi came to dinner. She took the children and I see them every alternate weekend. The financial settlement was amicable. She lives with someone else now.

I'm with Jade. I met her about three months after Jessica left. We've been together for four years this September. We are getting married in June. Our first baby is due in October. Oh yes, I'm sure you will want to know, Jack and Heidi are married and, like us, are living happily ever after.

*   *   *

Alice

It was a nice evening. The summer sun was settling down in the west and the flowers eased themselves to sleep in the stillness of the night. My garden was suffering a little from the lack of rain this summer and anxious weatherman made it feel worse. Rose petals littered the dark soil I'd worked up in the spring and, though dying, seemed pleased at having been given a last chance to reflect the beauty heaven had bestowed on them.

It was nearly six-thirty. Alice had spent the last two hours getting ready. I had long learned that there was no point chasing her. Urgency was something she found difficult to cope with. I wondered how she coped at work but, unlike me, I never once heard her complain.

She always looked radiant. I never tired of looking at her and, as many a song goes, wondered what she had ever seen in me. She was magnificent; dark auburn hair that she frequently spoilt with tints offered by her effeminate hairdresser who took advantage of her fear of growing old.

I smiled at the thought of what the bedroom might look like; dozens of discarded dresses that she would spend half an hour tidying up when we got home, tired and a little drunk, and I would wait for her, impatient for her to come to bed.

Although sadly she had stopped undressing in front of me, depriving me of the pleasure I had enjoyed for a while after we got married, I would hold my breath to hear the sound of her changing in the en suite bathroom that had been such a godsend in the heady days of our youth. She was a dream, then. Maybe she still was. Her pale white skin that didn't like the sun was translucent, and her veins; delicate blue rivers that flowed underneath the mist of skin, resonated with life like an opal on fire.

We were expected at seven-thirty and had an hour's journey ahead of us. There were enough speed cameras on the roads to prevent shortening the journey time even if I was able to recall the recklessness of my youth. We had both mellowed, although I knew I was happier than Alice in accepting it. For me it meant having someone to come home to and the tenderness of the spoon position to lullaby me to sleep.

I looked at my watch; it was coming up to seven and still no sign of Alice. I thought about calling up to her, instinct never left me, but I had the presence of mind to decide against it for all the reasons I've mentioned. A cool autumn breeze picked up which I used as an excuse to go indoors.

I walked into the sitting room of our comfortable semi-detached suburban house, switched on the television and began the, by now, involuntary channel hopping that accompanied waiting. Reality show after reality show flicked by before I settled on a travel show to numb the increasingly vulnerable senses, the same way as musak did in a waiting room.

'Sorry I'm late,' said Alice rushing in, 'you should have called, I didn't realise the time.'

'Don't worry,' I said, switching off the television, leading her to the front door, grabbing the car keys on the way.

We left. The journey, predictable, ate up the hour of our lives allotted to it. The radio played songs increasingly few of which I remembered. We talked in short sentences, but mostly, as was want these days, I listened to Alice. My responses were adequate, allowing Alice to calm herself for the evening ahead. She was always apprehensive about going to parties.

'Darling, you haven't once said whether I look alright.'

That was my cue; an opportunity we both enjoyed. I recalled Eric Clapton's legacy to our marriage with affection, 'My darling, you look wonderful tonight.'

'Are you sure? I haven't got too much make-up on, have I?'

'No my darling, you look as beautiful as the first day I saw you.'

'Are you sure?'

'Yes of course.'

We were late, but thankful the invitation was not for dinner. The party, thrown by John and Mary, was to celebrate their return from a mission in South Africa. They had been away for two years and needed to welcome themselves back to friends left behind. Still bronzed, despite two months of an English summer, they looked as if they had just returned from holiday in the Caribbean. There were already a lot of people flowing into the three ground floor rooms of their detached house. Snacks were laid out on the dining table and, in the corner of another room a bar had been set up with a mix of wines, and thoughtfully, soft drinks and juices for those of us wary about drinking and driving.

There were lots of new faces mixed in with old acquaintances rather than friends. We waded through rooms, wine glasses in hand, looking to see if there were others we shouldn't miss.

Standing on his own, leaning against a wall, was a young man in his late thirties who nodded a greeting to me as I walked past.

'Hello, lovely evening,' I said.

'Yes, it is isn't it?'

'My name's Hubert.'

'Hello, mine's Geoff. '

'Oh, and this is my wife, Alice.'

'Hello Alice, very nice to meet you.'

Geoff was charming. He was tall and handsome in an unreliable sort of way; the sort of young man that vanity prevents engagement in relationships of any permanence. I had met them in my youth with envy. Girls were always attracted to them and Alice was no exception. He encouraged her, flirting with a casual air of confidence. I watched myself uncontrollably drift away from the conversation to take the position of observer. Her questions became provocative as she tried to engage him.

'So, why are you on your own?'

'Alice!'

'What?' she almost shouted turning to me, visibly irritated by the intrusion.

'I don't think that's a fair question.'

'Why?'

'Well,' I struggled, smiling apologetically for Geoff's benefit, which he ignored. Alice had succeeded. Geoff was engaged. She left me struggling and turned back to Geoff.

'Well?'

'Well, Alice,' he said with a laugh, 'I suppose I just haven't found the right person yet.'

'I can't believe that. Someone like you *(I noticed the emphasis on 'you')* must have at least a hundred of girls chasing after them.'

'Alice,' I tried again to stop her.

'What? It's true. Darling, why don't you get me a refill? Oh yes, and Geoff too...another red, Geoff?'

'Thanks, I'm ok.'

'Don't be silly by the time he comes back you'll be finished.'

I was still standing there trying to confirm what I was meant to do.

'Go on then,' said Alice.

Walking off to get the drinks I tried to remember whether it was her third or fourth glass of wine. Whatever it was, the wine was getting to her, but I knew I was too late to do anything about it. Tomorrow she'd have a hangover which, like a rainy day, would ease the pressure of finding something to do on Sunday. Waiting in the queue for drinks I heard her laughter over the general din and felt the faint pangs of jealousy which thankfully didn't last long.

'Hello, Hubert.'

I looked around to see John. It was nice to have a chat. He obviously had a wonderful time in South Africa and, although glad to be back, it was clear they were both sad to leave. He relived adventures with the dramatic exaggeration of recollection and I enjoyed them too, vicariously, as is often the fate of those who fall into the routine of life at an early age. When

John left me I found other friends and quite forgot about the drinks I had been sent to fetch. I looked around once or twice to find Alice, but couldn't find her. I assured myself she was ok and moved among old friends, catching up on what was new in their lives. It was fun. It must have been over an hour before there was a respite when I remembered the drinks and made an effort to find my wife.

I was surprised, and a little annoyed, to find her still talking with Geoff.

'Oh, there you are. I thought you'd left me,' she laughed.

'Sorry, darling.'

She ignored my apology.

'I'm lucky to have found Geoff otherwise I would have been all alone. You see Geoff,' she said turning to him, 'that's what husbands are like. I am sure you wouldn't be like that though.'

'Oh no Alice, I'm sure your husband isn't like that.'

'Don't you believe it! He's impossible to live with. I don't know what I ever saw in him.'

I smiled apologetically at Geoff, but he ignored it, staring instead at Alice.

'Well, he said, 'we all make mistakes!' and laughed unmistakably like the gigolo I thought he certainly was.

'Come on Alice, I think we'd better be going.'

'No Hubert. I'm NOT ready. I am having such a nice time. Why don't you go and speak to someone else instead of spoiling it for me.'

Embarrassed, I left them to get myself a drink. I'd already had a glass of wine which is what I allowed myself when I was driving home, but I decided another glass wouldn't hurt. I mingled a little, all the time feeling angry, wishing I could leave her at the party and go home.

I hated Alice at such times. I don't know why she was like that. She knew that I didn't like it. I hated the way she flirted with anyone who would indulge her, acting like an old tart! A couple of glasses of wine and she would be charming with anyone who paid her any attention. She would put on an act of a suffering wife, swearing, for added effect, that no-one could imagine what she had to put up with. And what did she have to put up with.... a husband, foolish enough to love her enough to never look at another woman, let alone flirt with someone.... a husband who always complimented her on how beautiful she looked even when she looked miserable.... a husband who always told her how much he loved her and, who really did! I may have been sulking, but felt justified.

'So there you are! Where did you get to? I've been looking for you everywhere. I mean, for goodness sakes, who leaves his wife all alone at a party? I don't know why I come with you if you're going to abandon me.'

'So Geoff left you, did he?' I replied, still sulking.

'Geoff left hours ago and, I've been on my own for ages,' she replied, clearly not picking up what I'd said. I was feeling better.

'I'm sorry, darling, so are you ready to go?'

'Yes darling. I think we'd better. I'm a bit tired and I think I may have drunk a little too much. That beastly Geoff kept refilling my glass even though I kept telling him that I didn't want any more.'

I wasn't angry anymore.

We took our leave and drove home. Alice didn't say anything all the way home. I suppose it was the alcohol. I didn't switch on the radio. After the noise of the party we both needed some peace and quiet. The journey home was shorter as it always is.

In bed, I was glad to be home again. Alice turned away and I snuggled up with my arm around her; my left hand holding hers. I tried to listen to hear her fall asleep, but could tell by the sound of her breathing she was still awake.

'Goodnight darling,' I said, hiding my face in her hair.

'Goodnight.'

I breathed in the smell of shampoo mixed with alcohol and cigarette smoke. It felt wonderful to be home. I was just about to fall asleep when Alice spoke.

'Darling, you know that Geoff?

I winced. I'd almost forgotten about him.

'Mmm.'

'At first he was charming, and then, you know what he said? He said he couldn't see how a beautiful woman like me could be happy settled in suburbia when there was so much to see in the world. Do you think we've missed out?'

'No, darling, we have each other.'

'I know, but there so much we haven't seen. Did you hear John and Mary talk of the fun they had in South Africa?'

'Are you sad you married me?'

Alice turned and gave me a kiss.

'No darling. I'm glad I have you,' she replied, giving me a kiss.

'I love you, Alice.'

'I know darling....but, you know, sometimes I wonder what it might have been like to see more of the world, experience other things. I mean, it's been a good life, but there's a lot that's passed us by, don't you think?'

She was right, of course, and there's nothing I can say that would make it any easier. I thought of all the things I'd like to have done.

'We can't have everything,' I said with a sigh.

'Yes, I suppose so, never mind. Goodnight darling.'

'Goodnight.'

As we resumed our 'spoon' position I thought about what Alice had said, and shrugged it off as being only natural. Our lives had been spent rushing around trying to make ends meet, bringing up the children, and when we'd finally got the comfort we'd spent our whole lives trying to get, the children had left home. I always thought it would be wonderful to have Alice all to myself as it had been in that first year of our marriage, but it's never the same and, I don't think Alice ever got over the children leaving home.

I felt sorry for her and myself too. Sorry that there were all those things that we'd dreamed of doing and somehow, along the way, had run out of time. Now I feared losing Alice. I couldn't imagine what I'd do if I lost her.

I heard her breathing calm into the familiar rhythm of sleep and kissed her gently on the back of her neck. 'Best leave to dreams all

that we might have had,' I thought as I too tried
to fall asleep.

*   *   *

The Dream of Angels

Siobhan

I think there are words that describe how I feel, important words, long and difficult. When I'm hungry, all I need to say is, 'I'm hungry,' and everyone understands. If I'm tired, I say, 'I'm tired,' and I can go to bed without answering any questions.

I find it difficult explaining why I like something because people interrupt me and I forget what I wanted to say. They use long and complicated words which I don't understand. They like to talk a lot. It's for my own good they say. They're always teaching me or asking me questions! Sometimes I want to tell them to 'bog off' but I can't. I don't know why I get angry when people ask me questions.

People ask me what I want to do most of all. 'I'm not sure,' I say. I don't tell them I'd like to run away. Leaving the hand that always holds me I want to run away to my hotel.

It would be my hotel. My dad can buy it for me. I'd live in a huge penthouse with a bed and a bedside lamp. All the birthday presents I've ever had would be neatly placed on shelves on the walls around the room. There would be a big television I could watch from my bed. There would be a games room, a relaxing room, a quiet room, a swimming pool with an instructor to teach me how to swim, a mini gym with another instructor and, a dining room. There would be a television in every room except the relaxing room where I would read, chill out, and think about all the stuff people think about. I'd also have an office where I'd do the paperwork, deal with the finances (whatever that is), find out what the people in my hotel are up to, and sort things out. When the people would have arguments I'd tell them to cool down, and sort it out. If they don't, they'd be out of the hotel, I mean my hotel. I don't like people arguing. I don't argue I just get angry sometimes.

I'd be important in my hotel. I'd be the boss! Everyone would listen to me, depend on me and I would help people, not the other way around.

On weekdays I'd invite my teachers and my friends from college and, on the weekends, my family could come to stay.

I would order whatever I wanted; pizza, a sandwich, a drink, crisps, some chocolate biscuits, anything! I'd take my bed with me because I like my bed. I'd tell someone to paint my bedroom pink and, have all my soft Disney toys with me all neatly around the room. I'd let Minnie come too. I'm not jealous of her anymore...well, not much. Anyway, she was nice to me when I met her in Disneyland, so it's ok. Buddy can stay in bed with me as he's done ever since I was a baby. He's as old as I am.

I'll tell everyone what to do and not the other way around. It's not fair! I don't like holding hands, but I have to.

I don't like answering questions while I'm walking because I have to concentrate. I've told them, but they always forget. They keep asking me questions to make me reply. They're not mean, just forgetful. They're family. I don't mind, but sometimes I forget I have to concentrate on walking, lose my balance, and fall. I hate falling. My stupid right foot comes in front of my left foot and makes me fall. Sometimes I hurt myself and, when no-one's looking, I cry.

I have a friend at college who comes on facebook. His name is Ben. Sometimes he's stupid. I send him a message on chat and he doesn't reply. I wait for him to reply but he doesn't. I get so angry sometimes. But it's ok. I've got other friends as well. There's Emma, Lucy, Hayley and Sonia. Oh yes, and Caroline too...and Cheryl. That's all I think. They come online too, sometimes. I like my iPad. I don't like people borrowing it. They can borrow it when I go to bed. I don't mind it then.

I love my big sister and my mum. I love my dad too, when he's near me. He embarrasses me sometimes. Like the time when we were going on a college trip and he kissed me good-bye in front of all my friends!

I like my teachers too. They like me. I hate maths though. I like reading. I like watching television too. I used to go to a youth club, but I can't go anymore because I'm too old. I miss it. Sometimes, I cry. I don't mean to.

When I was little I used to go shopping with my grandma. And, sometimes, we'd pass shops with models of disabled people holding a collection box chained to something. My grandma would always give me some money to put in the box. The money was for people who need help. When my grandma went to heaven they took the boxes away. I remember the boxes when I see old people or people in wheelchairs. I'm very lucky I can walk.

I don't like people telling me I should go to bed, especially when I'm playing a game. I like playing solitaire. They tell me to go to bed and I reply 'in a minute'. Then they tell me ten minutes have passed since I said 'in a minute,' and I tell them 'I'll go up in a minute,' and on and on, until I get fed up, leave the game unfinished, and go up to bed.

I'm not a baby. I don't need people to tell me what to do all the time. 'Do this, do that, do this, do that,' or whatever!

Ok, I'm tired. I think I'll go to bed now. I'll put on my socks because I get cold at night. I'll put my hands together like this; put them under my chin and go to sleep. I'll talk to myself for a while before I fall asleep. I talk about anything really. Sometimes I talk to my friends, or my teachers, or Mickey, or my mum, or my sister and, sometimes, my dad. But he's not here. I miss him sometimes. It makes me sad.

Other things make me sad too. Sometimes, when I'm sad, I cry. Alright, I'm tired. I'm going to switch off the light now. I'll speak to you tomorrow. Goodnight.

Rapunzel

When I was little, six or seven, my mother used to brush my hair before I went to bed. She used to brush my long blonde hair humming a lullaby as I watched her in the mirror. When she'd finished, she would make two long ringlets that would hang like Christmas decorations on either side of my face. She said I looked like an angel. She said that if she'd had long blonde hair like mine, my dad would still be here today. She told me he's gone to heaven. I didn't understand that at the time. I couldn't understand why he had to go to heaven because my mum didn't have hair like mine. I knew not to ask because that would make her cry. My mum had short black hair with single white strands that escaped the colour she used to stop her hair going grey.

When I'd get into bed my mum would read to me. She read 'Rapunzel,' my favourite fairy story, every night. My mother told me that when I grew up a prince would come and take me away. At first I was frightened, but then she told me he'd only take me away if I wanted to go.

At first I told my mother I'd never leave her. When I got older I'd say, if the prince came to take me away I'd only go if he'd let me take my mum with me. Later, I promised I wouldn't live far away and that I'd come to see her often. I always liked that story and promised myself that if I had a daughter I'd call her Rapunzel.

When I was little, I told my best friend at school I had a prince who was waiting for me to grow up. She told the other boys and girls in my class and they were horrible to me. They made me cry and I promised to tell my prince when he came. I'd tell him of the cruel boys, and tell him to hit them, especially Jonathan. Not the girls though, because boys can't hit girls. I forgot about that when I went to university because boys weren't horrible to me anymore.

I knew I was right to wait for my prince. I recognised him immediately. He was exactly as I imagined him. He had long, dark, wavy black hair that fell on his forehead. He had light green eyes just visible through horn rimmed glasses that he wore like Corbusier. He was tall, thin, caring and shy. I waited. I knew he'd notice me. I waited a whole term. I went to parties with my friends. Boys would come up to talk to me. If they asked for more, I'd tell them I had a boyfriend, but wouldn't say who he was. I saw him at a party once, but before I got close enough, he left. It was two days before the end of term. I promised mum I'd go home for the holiday and nearly didn't, just in case I'd see him again. His name was Robert Furst.

When I went home my mum asked me about boys. I didn't tell her about Robert. I wanted to. I would when the time was right. I said I didn't have a boyfriend because I was waiting for my prince.

Robert became my boyfriend almost immediately after I got back to university. I saw his parents at the next holiday and he came to see mum the one after that. We took a little flat together while at university.

Shortly after we started working, my mum gave us some money to buy a little flat of our own. It was a small flat on the top floor, overlooking a garden. I told him I would grow my hair long and he could call up to me, 'Rapunzel, Rapunzel,' and I'd let down my hair. It was our place in which to live happily ever after. And we did for nearly a year before he left me. I wanted to run after him but I couldn't. Sitting in front of the mirror, brushing my hair as mum did all those years ago, I talk to her. Sometimes I talk to her in bed. I wonder whether she can hear me in heaven.

Other things make me sad too. Sometimes, when I'm sad, I cry. Alright, I'm tired. I'll have a bath tomorrow. It doesn't matter because I sleep alone. I'm going to switch off the light now. I'll speak to you tomorrow. Goodnight.

Dad

I fell in love with her. She came out of a fairy story. Beautiful long blonde hair, grey eyes, and lips that smiled at the touch of a button that she kept locked in her handbag. Like a chameleon, she changed colour depending on the seasons or, when I noticed, the time of day. I wanted someone to love and she came along. Quiet, pensive, uncertain, waiting for someone to rekindle the flames of desire, she searched for him in dreams. There were moments when she was physically so close to me that I shuddered with delight, with desperation. I so wanted to take her up in my arms and hold her. A tight embrace leaving us gasping for air in between 'stuck' kisses sucking on each other like loaches, hungry, draining, consuming, digging deeper with tongues sliding over each other trying to reach distant chasms which, even with mouths wide open, we could not reach. At such moments I felt faint, intoxicated by her fragrance, a blend so very personal to her.

I dreamed of her while she dreamed of another. I had put my ghosts to rest but hers were still alive. She clung to them believing that if she'd let go, life itself would leave her, while they in turn struggled to wrench themselves free.

Rapunzel, Rapunzel, let down your beautiful, long blonde hair and let me crawl into

110

the dark recesses of your heart to light a candle and say a prayer. Come close to me, innocent of my desire, and let me breathe you once again. But it was too late. In memory of her lost love she cut her hair and so there were no locks for me to climb. Our loneliness was complete, symmetrical, unrequited, and therefore never free of desire; our consummation of emptiness.

'Dad, what do dream of?'

'Of many things, my darling.'

'Like what?'

'I dream of you.'

'Ok, ok, what do you want?'

'All your love.'

'I knew you were going to say that!'

There was a pause while we both dreamed of ordinary lives; cooking, cleaning, shopping, waiting and love.

'Dad, can I ask you a question?'

'Yes of course, my angel.'

'Do you dream of love?'

'I try not to.'

'Why?'

'It hurts.'

'Does it always hurt?'

'Yes, my darling.'

'Why?'

'Because, my angel, falling in love doesn't make life any easier.'

Other things make me sad too. Sometimes, when I'm sad, I cry. Alright, I'm tired. I'm going to switch off the light now. I'll speak to you tomorrow. Goodnight.

Siobhan

Sitting on the pebble beach in Hove, a mile or two from Brighton on the south coast of England, staring out to sea, I listen to waves bringing in shells for me to collect. I know the sea shells are there, but I can't walk to them.

I see children playing in the water, splashing each other and screaming with laughter. The one's I would play with are quietly making little sand castles just out of reach of the water.

My family are walking near enough to the water to get their feet wet. I'm home alone in my little world of summer sunshine. The sea gulls scream at each like the children do in the refectory at college where I have my lunch. I sit with my friend, usually. Our helper leaves us with our packed lunches while she has her break. The sea gulls are hungry. They're always hungry. Not like us. I have to eat my four little squares of sandwich, my chocolate, and drink my juice; otherwise my mum will tell me off. Sometimes Ben joins us and asks for one of my sandwich squares which I give him. My mum doesn't always ask me whether I ate everything, which is good because then she doesn't find out I've given some away.

It's a nice day. It's hard work going out, but I suppose it's better than being bored at home, especially when either my sister or my mum are watching something on television. When they watch television I usually play a game on my iPad or go on facebook to see if my friends are online. It's sad when there's no-one online.

I can see a dog running on the sea shore. I hope he doesn't come near me. I'm scared of dogs because I don't know what they're going to do next. They might bite me.

I'm hot. When someone comes, I'll ask for a drink.

They asked me whether I wanted to join them on the beach. I said I was happy sitting on the bench on the promenade, but they insisted which is why I'm here. I'm on my own, but that's ok. I don't mind. I'll wait for them. My dad is walking with my sister. My mum is looking for shells with my cousin. I'm sure she'll bring me some shells too. If she doesn't I'll send her back to get some.

I can see a ship, actually two, no, three, no four....oh I don't know. I don't care. I wish I could run around like the other children, but my stupid legs won't let me. My legs are hurting. I need to stand. I don't want to try to stand because I'll fall over. The children are playing football. The boys are being horrible to the girls. I don't think they should be horrible. I think they should let the girls have fun too.

There's a mum with a baby. The baby's crying. I like babies. They're nice. I like playing with them when they're not crying. Adults are nice too. They're nice to me. My dad brought me a book, but I don't want to read it. People might hear me reading it. I can't help reading aloud. My mum and sister make fun of me when I read. They say the neighbours can hear me. I don't like them saying that. It's not my fault I read aloud.

I love my sister. She loves me, too. That means she doesn't just love me, she loves my mum and dad as well. She's going to get married. I don't like thinking about it. Mum says she'll have to go away. The house will feel very empty. I'll miss her. It'll make me sad. I'll cry.

I don't think I'll get married. Ben's nice. He looks after me when I'm at college. He's not my boyfriend. I think he likes me. Our mums took us to the shopping centre and we had hot chocolate. We talked about college and stuff.

When we came home I was tired. I didn't want any dinner so I had a sandwich and a drink. I had to wait a little after my sandwich before I could go up to bed. It was a nice day. I think I'll have a bath tomorrow. Today, I can't be bothered. Buddy won't mind.

I walk up the stairs carefully because I'm tired. I don't want to fall. My Mum shouts to me to be careful. I shout back 'I am!' My dad says he'll come to put me to bed. He'll be up in a minute, after I've been to the toilet.

I'm sitting on the bed when my dad comes into my bedroom. He helps me put on my socks and tucks me in. He sits by my side for a minute and then leans over to kiss me goodnight.

'I love you my baby.'

'I love you.'

'What are you going to dream of tonight, my darling?'

'Nothing,' she says, and then, quietly, a smile creeps across her face. 'I'll dream of running away.'

'And leave me all on my own?' I say.

'I'll come to see you.'

'I'll be sad, my angel, I'll cry.'

'It's alright, dad, it's only a dream.'

114

'I know, but dreams sometimes come true.'

'Do other things make you sad?'

'No, my darling, only dreams make me sad. Sometimes, when I'm sad, I cry. Alright, I'm tired. I'm going to switch off the light now. I'll speak to you tomorrow. Goodnight.'

As I leave the room in the still of the night, with my angel in bed lying on her side, her hands clasped together in prayer tucked under her chin, I glance back to say goodnight.

'Goodnight,' she whispers.

'Love you.'

'Love you too.'

'Sweet dreams.'

'Dad?'

'Yes my angel.'

'I wish dreams would come true.'

'Me too.'

*   *   *

The illusion of love

J

It was unexpected when it came. The call I mean. I was sitting in my flat after a routine of cooking, eating, showering with self indulgence, clutching a mug of coffee already cold with indifference, and embracing the numbing effect of watching television with resignation, when I heard my phone register an SMS. I savoured the delight of guessing who it could be, holding back the curiosity that had a habit of ending up in disappointment. I ran through the names of friends.

My friends are categorised between those that send me an SMS, those that ring, and those still undeleted in the phone book even though it's been months, sometimes years, since we've been in touch.

In those days I considered friends that sent me a SMS a strange bunch. In the beginning I didn't forgive them for sending me an SMS when they could just as easily have called. I didn't like sending an SMS in reply. I could have called them back, I know, but somehow an SMS demands an SMS in return. Now, it's alright. I've got used to it and am guilty of much the same myself.

It was at a party that we met; one of those relationships that very much ended before it really began. I can't remember what brought us together, but I remember I had a wonderful time. We spent long enough for others to start rumours and, long enough for me to think there was something worth pursuing.

Dave came over with girlfriend and addressed us as one does a couple.

'Hi. Good party. Why aren't you guys on the dance floor?'

I don't know why, but I was pleased they thought we were together. I half listened to Dave, straining to hear what the girls were talking about. It was hard to hear what they were saying with Freddie Mercury screaming to be set free in the background but, every time our eyes met, we shared an intimacy that was enough for my friends to think we were in love.

'So how long have you known each other?'

'Actually, Dave, they're not together,' said his girlfriend.

We smiled as best we could to hide the embarrassment and she left the three of us on some pretext which I can't remember.

'Sorry,' said Dave.

'That's alright, don't worry about it,' I said.

I think once we had both denied it so publically there didn't seem much of a future in having a relationship, so maybe that's why we didn't. She left an impression on me. I was surprised how much I thought of her having only met her once at the party.

It's debatable which is worse; the pain of losing the reality of what we have, or losing the chance of a relationship that never was. We dismiss the disappointment caused by the loss of what might have been as being silly, and yet, it was real for me. We met a couple of times after

117

the party, but she was clear in the way she behaved that we were only ever going to be friends. I suffered desperately at the time despite repeated unsuccessful attempts to convince myself that there was nothing lost because there had been nothing to lose in the first place.

I smiled with sadness when I read the message. It had been many months since we had stopped seeing each other.

It doesn't often happen that I imagine I've found someone to fall in love with, but when it does and then it doesn't work out, it hurts. She had moved on from leaving an acquaintance in me to a boyfriend in someone else. I, having accepted defeat, had put it down to one of those unfulfilled desires that memories are made of.

I wondered why she wanted to speak to me now. I hoped that her relationship hadn't gone sour since I don't find any pleasure in picking up someone on the rebound. I rather hoped that she, secure in the safety of a new relationship, felt confident enough to search me out.

'Hi, haven't spoken for a while, wondered whether you fancy dinner sometime?' read the SMS.

I wanted to say 'No thanks. I don't want to have dinner with you! What's the point? Why do you want to have dinner with me? What would your boyfriend say? Isn't he the jealous type? I would be. Thanks, but no thanks!', but didn't. I thought about what to write for it a long time but in the end settled for a simple reply.

'I would love to. The weekend is best for me. Tell me a Saturday night when you might be free.'

I sent the message and tried to stop myself waiting for a reply. None came that evening, though there was one the next morning.

'Saturday evenings are difficult. What about Sunday lunch?'

I was glad she didn't ring me. I wouldn't have known what to say. Months had passed with nothing and now Sunday lunch!

I didn't want to have lunch on Sunday because the evening would torment me with replays of the conversation we had over lunch. I decided it would have to be an evening so that I would come home and go to sleep.

I wasn't ready to reply the next morning. I needed more time and took it. After all, if nothing came of it, it wouldn't matter. Was it eight months of indifference already? Anyway, it's not nice to flirt with someone in a relationship. That's what breaks up relationships and I think starting a new relationship born of destruction is difficult. I didn't want to hurt her. It wouldn't be fair.

I thought a long time about the response, nearly all morning, and then it came to me. I asked her to choose between two dates, a couple of weeks away. I wanted to make sure she understood that I was not desperate, that I felt nothing. I wanted her to understand that I could be busy too.

'Ok, at the moment I have two dates free in the next three weeks. Let me know if they are any good; a week next Wednesday or the following Monday.'

I didn't want them close to the weekend because I didn't want to spend the weekend thinking about her.

It was cold. I felt a chill in the air. I felt the shudder of death passing me by. It was a death remembered. I didn't want to die again. The SMS reminded me of the pain I felt. The reply was swift.

'Thanks. Wednesday sounds good. You choose where?'

I had plenty of time. The date had been fixed. I let time pass by. She waited and I let her wait. On the Sunday evening, with three days to go, I decided to think about a venue.

I wasn't playing hard to get. There was nothing on offer and nothing I wanted. It was just something to look forward to. The longer I didn't reply, the longer I could plan. Once, I wouldn't have needed to think about it, but now, things were different. I would have loved to take her somewhere romantic, but now she was not alone. I finally decided on a place. It was the venue of our first date after the party, a non-descript café along a road that had nothing memorable about it, apart from meeting her there. I imagined it as a romantic epitaph to the promise of a relationship that didn't happen. She suggested somewhere else which was fine because I didn't really care.

𝒥𝒥

The restaurant was crowded and we had to wait for our table. The waitress suggested the bar and I offered to get the drinks. I stood at the bar waiting to be served.

My mind was in turmoil. What was I doing there? I really didn't want to do this. She sat on a bar stool smiling each time I affected the disappointment of not getting the attention of the barman. I didn't want to be there. It was far too noisy. I wasn't even hungry. I wanted to go up to her, admit this was a bad idea, and go home. I didn't want to play the game anymore. I smiled to myself as I thought how melodramatic it would be if I went up to her and said I was sorry, told her that this was all a mistake, lead her astonished out of the restaurant, kiss her on the cheek and go home. What a fitting end to a relationship that had never been! Ah, what an exit!

Irritated at not getting the attention of the barman, I went up to her and asked whether it would be alright if we found somewhere else. The plan hadn't worked. My mind was no longer in control. I was not in control. It was contagious. She seemed flustered. She wasn't smiling anymore.

'Where do you want to go?' she asked.

'I don't know. Let's just get out of here.'

She got off the bar stool and we left. There was bound to be something nearby. I realised after taking a few paces along the road that I hadn't bothered to tell the waitress that we were leaving.

As we walked along side by side I realised how cold it was. I wished she was someone else so that I could have held her hand, warm in the knowledge that I was with someone I wanted to be with. I wanted to get this dinner over and done with and go home to the emptiness of my flat. At least that emptiness would be real, something that I had, packed with a healthy dose of routine, learned to live with. I didn't know what to talk about. The weather seemed too commonplace. I needed some answers so that I would know how to behave. Why had she sent the SMS? Was there hope? Regret perhaps? Even pity! Any one of those reasons would have helped. I would have known how to behave. Although I know how to react to hope or regret, I was still uncertain of 'pity'. Pride wouldn't allow me to accept pity, her pity. I had enough of my own nurtured through many lonely nights. I knew I couldn't ask. I wanted to but the moment wasn't right. I knew there would be a moment when silence would betray the fact that we had talked about everything that politeness would allow.

It was too cold to walk any further so I suggested the first restaurant I saw with empty tables. We were shown to our seats with affectation and allowed to remove our own coats before taking our seats.

'Well, this is a nice place.'

The small talk continued.

'Yes.'

We took our seats at a table set for two, opposite each other. I always felt that such a seating arrangement was cold as no effort is required by either person to steal a glance. Maybe, that's the point.

We ordered our drinks, making them complicated so that the waiter would help us delay the necessity to have a conversation. The start was dire and, if the evening was to continue as it had started, we were destined to exhaust ourselves with boredom.

The menus were handed to us and I read everything there was before choosing a main course that I guessed would not be too long in coming.

'Not having a starter?'

'No thanks, I might have dessert later. But do have one yourself if you would like.'

I knew she wouldn't. I couldn't face the thought of a long dinner. We had agreed a late start. Enough time to go home and change but still eight-thirty on a Wednesday evening meant that there were only about two hours to kill.

The waiter took our order and left us with our drinks. We drank our drinks, the drinks more interesting than the conversation.

'So how have you been?'

'Fine, what about you? Busy?'

'Well, sort of. What have you been doing?'

I half listened to what she was saying. I wondered what it was that had attracted me to her in the first place. I had seen her face before. The memory of it was still fresh. Her hair as I remembered it, her pug nose slightly turned up as it had been, her use of make-up still very personal but loud enough to be noticed. I remembered all these things as I did the determination of wanting to be in control of a world that had the habit of slipping away. I fancied she must be tired of running away but I'm not sure whether that perception was the projection of my masculinity; the need to save a damsel in distress!

I had thought about these kaleidoscope features so many times a long time ago, and now they offered nothing more than the memory of someone dear to me that I had lost somewhere. Those memories hurt. I had to stop. I wasn't going to let them hurt me anymore. I dismissed

123

her endearing features as luxuries that I couldn't afford.

I followed her neck down her throat to where there should have been the necklace that wasn't there, around her ears to the studs she was wearing when I saw her last, and then down to her sweater, revealing breasts, modestly enclosed in functional wrapping that allowed no erotic thoughts. It would have helped to be vulgar but my gaze darted back to her lips. I looked for the imperfection of lip gloss that had distracted me in a previous life, wondering what a kiss might taste like. I imagined the faint taste of alcohol she had been drinking, the moistness of her tongue and the taste of lip gloss which would have been enough to make me giddy.

I would in other circumstances have been proud, imagining how my kiss would make her helpless, but there is something about having lost, failure in love, that makes arrogance unconvincing.

'So, what about your Saturdays? What makes you so busy?'

The question hurt but I was prepared for the answer. Go on I dare you, say it! 'Orgasmic thrashing about until the stupor of love making leaves us in a daze. Every Saturday night, wild fantasies played out in pure uncensored pornography! Gosh, you would've had to have been there to believe it!'

'Nothing much. Same old usual. What about you? What's new?'

'Well, something strange happened recently. My mother has a friend.'

I wasn't sure what to say.

'That's nice,' was the involuntary reply.

'Well it's a bit strange. It's been eight years since my father died. I suppose I didn't expect it. I just answered my mother's mobile. I've done it in the past so it was the natural thing to do. It was a man. He wanted to speak to my mother. I asked him who he was and he said he was a friend. I called my mother. She told him she was busy and hung up. I didn't say anything. I didn't know what to say. She said it was just someone she met. There was nothing in it, just a friend.'

'Well, she is a woman and, there is nothing worse than loneliness no matter what your age is.' I imparted worldly wisdom. I, who had never understood the world, was imparting worldly wisdom! I was good at that. My nervousness at intimacy gave way to confidence. I always find it easy to be objective about someone else's life.

'I just can't imagine her having a friend.' She said it with a smile that one reserves for strangers, but as I stared, she looked away, embarrassed.

'Do you think your mother can imagine you?' I sneered. God, it sounded so hypocritical. I could be honest but it sounded cruel. And then, suddenly feeling vulnerable I said, looking down at my drink, 'You know, I can't imagine you.'

She laughed. It was a laugh of embarrassment. I was embarrassed too, embarrassed at having revealed too much. But it was true. I had thought about it, in fact, ever since she told me she couldn't meet me anymore because she had a boyfriend. I tried to imagine what they would be like together. I imagined the sort of relationship that develops over time, the slow realisation that it was better to be with someone rather than be on your own and, having found someone, to make the best of it. Good or bad, it was still better than nothing, the loneliness of scraping through life which, at best, only had a semblance of meaning.

'Have you tried?' she asked. That was a good response. I expected her to ignore the remark or act as if she didn't hear it. It took me off-guard so I resorted to the truth.

'Yes,' I said.

'I can't imagine you either.'

'Either what?'

She blushed, and I think I must have done too. We both looked down at our drinks once more and, after a moment, looked up in sync. We both smiled as if we had shared a secret but realised that we didn't have to be ashamed. We were suddenly transformed into strangers passing through the night, travellers with nothing to lose. The conversation could be as degenerate as we wanted it to be and it wouldn't matter because we would never see each other again. It would be an affair without complications, without remorse, without expectations, without any of the dangers that could turn our lives upside down.

The waiter came to take our order. It was a welcome pause in the conversation. I watched her explain what she wanted. She took her time and the waiter did his job well. He listened patiently as I watched her performance. Finally, satisfied at her victory of having changed the main course beyond recognition of the creator of the menu, she handed the waiter over to me. I think he was worried that he might have to go through something similar with me which accounts for the smile he gave me for agreeing to have something already on the menu.

There was something endearing about what I had seen; a beautiful girl enjoying the indulgence that the world offers beautiful girls. And then I remembered she wasn't mine. I became angry with myself for the momentary relapse.

'If I said you are the most beautiful girl in the world, would you believe me?'

I could see her searching for an answer.

'You know you're not,' I said.

I waited for the effect of the answer to take hold. I think it took her by surprise because she was still searching for a way to respond.

'I don't think I have ever seen a girl that I could say was the most beautiful girl in the world,' I continued.

I wondered whether that would soften the blow. I was playing games. I had every right to. She was too. Why the dinner? Why me? Why now after all this time? I was exhausted. I couldn't find the answers. I was hurting her, the last thing I wanted to do and yet, she was still here. Why didn't she just get up and go? It was clearly a mistake and yet we were caught, something that an ill conceived SMS had started which had to be gone through.

'Yes, I know you don't think I am the most beautiful girl in the world. You told me the last time we met. I told you then that I wouldn't believe you.'

I was surprised she remembered something that I had forgotten. Did she think I

127

cared? I had wanted to love her. I had needed to love her at the time. I had wanted to be with her. I had decided that she was going to be my salvation. I was going to dream her into the angel that I had always wanted. Oh God! How I had wanted her to be the one. When she told me she had found a boyfriend and wanted me to meet him I was hurt. I hated myself for being myself. I hated myself for making the same mistake again. I had been betrayed, and yet, the strangest thing was that there was nothing to betray except in my imagination. How could I have made the same mistake again? I had made it so many times before and still persisted in making them. I was stupid to think that the girl that would attract me would also be attracted by me. I wanted to tell her how I had felt; her stupid smile, those eyes that creased when she laughed, her hair that fell around her shoulders, and her lips that now hid those teeth that worked the fish into the digestible morsels she could swallow. How I wanted to kiss her neck, breathing in the fragrance that intoxicated me the very first time I met her at the party. They were all precious to me, once. I had wanted to write verse that would be worthy of a first love experienced by a thirteen year old, but that was all a long time ago. I was done with all that nonsense.

'Well, I suppose you are clever then! Not like stupid girls who believe compliments are free.'

The food came and I realised I was hungry. It tasted good too. I ate with relish. I used the food to give me the break in conversation that we both needed. We ate in silence, looking up now and then with a smile, exaggerating the pleasure of eating.

'Did you ever give compliments that were free?'

The question sparked a quick scan of all the relationships I had been through and I responded with honesty. Compliments, when you know nothing is on offer, are always free.

'Yes, always. Always, that is, except once.'

'Who was that?'

'Someone, a long time ago but she's dead now.' I lied. She wasn't dead.

'I'm sorry.'

'I'm not.'

'You are angry with me.'

'No.' I lied.

'Did you love her?'

'No.' I lied.

I wondered whether she knew I loved her. I thought girls could always sense those sorts of things.

'You did love her didn't you?'

The pain of a reopened wound returned for a moment. I couldn't understand why she was so interested in someone else. She was the one I wanted to love. I tried to deflect the question.

'I don't think love is something that dies. It stays with you forever,' I said.

'I don't think so.'

I wanted to interrupt but she stopped me.

'It's the illusion of love that lasts forever, because love can't survive in the real world.'

I forgot what I wanted to say, repeating her answer slowly to myself and, just as gently as the lifting of the morning mist, her answer made me realise what was causing all the confusion that evening.

She had a boyfriend. Our relationship had never stepped across the threshold of reality. I was off limits. She had sent me away and, because of that, my illusion of her had survived. I loved her still. I had loved someone before her and still did, and yet I loved her too. The hypocrisy had come home to me. All I had ever thought about love; the dream that lasts forever, didn't mean much. I realised that I couldn't love her. I would have to accept she couldn't be mine. Only the illusion of love would remain. And in those lonely nights, when I looked for that something that was missing in my life, I would think of her. Someone I loved and, even if it was an illusion of love, it would sustain me when I needed it.

I was glad of it. I was glad that she would remain someone I'd dreamed of, never letting reality destroy the dream born of hope all those months and years ago.

We ordered dessert. The conversation turned to irrelevances. We laughed at jokes that neither would remember. The waiter brought the bill. She offered to pay. I said she couldn't. She insisted. I refused.

'Has a girl never paid?'

'Never,' I said.

'Never?' she asked.

I don't know why her question reminded me.

'Once.'

'Well, this will be the second time.'

She took the bill and paid. I watched her take the money from her purse but didn't say anything. She had won this evening. She had called my bluff. She knew I loved her. She knew I would always love her. She had seen through all my disguises. It was her victory. It was her privilege.

The waiter looked at me as she paid. I made a gesture of helplessness. As he walked away he turned and winked. I smiled.

I walked her to the bus stop and we waited with small talk. I kissed her goodbye on the cheek. I watched the bus take her away. I smiled to myself. The dinner had been important. The illusion needed sustenance and the dinner provided it. The illusion had been preserved. I walked home happy in the thought that I would be able to dream of her that night and, maybe any other night when I felt alone.

* * *

The Wife

I

I struggled when you asked me to write a love story. I told you they don't exist. You said if I really loved you I would write a story for you. That was last summer. I didn't give you the story you wanted because I didn't believe in it, love I mean. Don't get me wrong, I was happy with you. I think we both were...sort of. I don't know when, but something changed. I thought it was me, but when you suggested a trial separation, although surprised, I was relieved. It's nice not to feel guilty about being the one who broke up, especially on those nights when you just don't feel like sleeping on your own.

I'm not writing this story for you. You have gone. It's more like a diary or maybe an epilogue, if you like, to our relationship. A sort of what happened next. It has nothing to do with us really. It just so happened that it started with the end of our relationship. I think it's about love, but not the way you talked about it before you left.

I told you love is an illusion. Something you read about or imagine. Like tomorrow, something just out of reach. I think it helps if you've lost someone because it's easier to fantasise about a feeling you imagine existed when they were around. It's a cruel reality that makes us believe in love at first sight and living happily ever after, but I suppose we always will.

This love story, if it is one, is one that lives with the acceptance that, while the dream may be elusive, many of us are happy to make do with a lot less. So here goes...

♪♪

It was last summer. I had just come out of a relationship that ended without either of us realising what was happening and then it was too late. We decided to separate for a trial period to check whether we still wanted to be together when I realised something that had been lingering at the back of my mind. It wasn't that I was bored of her, but I needed something new. Not a new face, although looks always have something to do with it, but something exciting, more exciting than what we'd had in the six years we were together. It's ok, it was her idea. At least she gave me the chance to say it wasn't my fault for which I'm grateful.

Anyway, we left each other to find ourselves. She rang sometime later to ask how I was doing and I said 'great'. I joined a gym and, as if I was hell bent on having a heart attack, went four or five times a week. I started running too. At first I thought 'this is dumb' but, as I built up stamina, I felt great.

As far as new relationships were concerned, I felt I needed to take some time off. It was fun being single again. I met friends, went to parties, went on dates when I was able to persuade myself that nothing long term was expected and, by and large, succeeded in not having another break up.

133

I met Basil at a party. He was already pretty plastered when he introduced himself with a pat on the back which was a little harder than I was happy to appreciate. He, however, persisted and, by the time I left, had taken my number and promised to call. I didn't realise at the time he was married because he was flirting outrageously with an equally drunk brunette when I left him.

A couple of weeks later Basil invited me over for brunch. I didn't really want to go but, as I was increasingly spending more time on my own I decided to accept. He said I could bring someone. There wasn't anyone I particularly wanted to entertain so I went on my own.

They were really kind; Basil drank too much and his wife, Kate, a slight, plain looking woman, was charming. There must have been at least ten years between them which may be why he often teased her as if she was a child. She smiled at him indulgently and played the role of the hostess which was slightly exaggerated as if not entirely sure how much she should be doing. She wasn't at the party. I never asked why.

Basil had a loud laugh and, safe in the comfort of his own home, mixed his drinks knowing that no matter how drunk he became his wife would make sure he slept in his bed minus his shoes and maybe his trousers.

I was pacing myself because I knew from my experience of him at the party that I wouldn't be able to compete with Basil, and also because there was no-one to take me home and put me to bed.

'You know, she's always telling me to stop smoking. I mean, can't a man enjoy the simple pleasures of life. Now tell me Stu, do you think that's fair?'

'Come on Basil, she just doesn't want you to kill yourself.'

'Yeah well she used to smoke too. Smoked for twelve years. Only gave up so she could have something to have a go at me about.'

'That's not fair darling, I just want you to live a healthier life.'

'You see, what did I tell you? She just wants to have a go at me, that's all. I mean life is hard you know. I have to deal with all the shit they throw at me all bloody week and, when the weekend comes along, you know, TGIF and all that, I don't get a chance to have a hang-over in peace. Saturday morning, she's up with sun, slamming cupboards in the kitchen or having the kettle going on the pretext of making coffee and then, would you believe it, the clinking of the bloody cups and saucers. I mean, think about it, who the hell has coffee at home in a cup and saucer. A mug's good enough for me.'

'Well, don't drink too much on a Friday night, just for a change, that way maybe you can both enjoy a coffee together on Saturday morning.'

'Nah, I know why she does it. She just wants an excuse to go out with her friends. I wake up and there isn't a sound in the flat. My head feels like someone's shoeing horses and I get up only because I need to go to the loo. I have a piss, go to kitchen to get a glass of water and there is a note over the sink. If I was less awake it would have got soaked..................*gone out*, it says, *be back in the afternoon.* I then

135

realise, here we go again! I tell you mate, marriage isn't all it is cracked up to be.'

'OK, Basil. I think you're going a bit too far,' said Kate, clearly embarrassed.

'Yes, Basil, that's not fair!' I added.

'Well,' said Basil, winking at me! 'Maybe you're right; it does have its advantages.'

Basil leaned over and, shielding his face from Kate, gave me another wink to make sure I'd got the hint.

'No, Basil, that's not what I mean. After all, what made you get married in the first place? Love must have had something to do with it.'

'Yeah well, I love you,' he said, turning to Kate, 'it's just that you drive me crazy sometimes! I spend half my time waiting for you to come back from work or shopping trips with your girlfriends and, when you're home, all you do is complain about my smoking and drinking. I mean, I don't complain about you going out, do I?'

He poured himself another drink and then, remembering I was still there, filled up my glass too. He looked at me as if thinking about what to say next and then continued.

'Stu, I hope you don't mind me asking, but why did you two split up?'

There is something about alcohol that people feel gives them the right to discuss your skeletons. I didn't mind talking about it; in fact there were times when I actually wanted to talk about it.

'I don't know. We just decided to have a break. It was her idea,' I added in self defence, 'and at the time I thought, well, if that's what she wants to do there's no point trying to stop her. When it happened I realised it was the best for both of us. We've spoken a few times, but now there's not much to talk about.'

'Didn't you love her?'

'That's not a fair question. Of course I loved her, to begin with, but then something happened, and, well, you just don't feel the same. You try and remember what it was like to begin with, but no matter how hard you try, you can't see her as the same girl you met all that time ago. Sounds like a soap opera but you know soaps aren't so far from reality.'

'I know,' he said with exaggerated remorse, 'shit happens.'

I was on a roll and the alcohol was working for both of us.

'I mean take the two of you, what dreams do you have. After all you've been married for two years now. What did you decide was going to be your dream when you got married?'

'That's easy. We wanted to get married because we loved each other. And now, we're saving enough money to buy the house we've always wanted. You know I've always wanted a house in Esher with a swimming pool. Later on we'll have a couple of kids. It's simple really. A couple of more years and that's what I'll have.'

'So money is going to buy you happiness?' I asked, facetiously.

'Too bloody right,' he said, missing the point, 'I'm gonna be stinking rich; kids in private school, a car for the missus, the lot!'

'And what about you?' I asked, turning to Kate. She thought for a while, took a sip of her wine to buy her time and then looked up at me. I was surprised she took the question so seriously. I wasn't being provocative; I just wanted to give her a chance to speak.

'It's a hard question...I've got many dreams.'

I don't know why, but I felt her face betray an anguish which was far more than the question I'd asked should have caused. I should have stopped and blame the next question on alcohol.

'It's ok Kate, just one. It doesn't have to be your only one.'

'Aw, give it a rest Stu. Kate's dream is the same as mine,' and then turning to Kate, continued, 'I'm gonna give you the world. Remember, that's what I promised. And don't you worry sweetheart, I will. You just wait n see.'

Kate's face relaxed and a smile appeared. 'I know darling. I know you will.'

I didn't stay much longer. Basil was drunk, the conversation was becoming serious, and it was getting late. I had a long journey home. Although I'd been careful not to drink too much I was glad I was taking the train. Basil was too drunk to drive and Kate offered to drop me off at the train station. I did offer calling a mini cab, but Kate insisted and I was too tired to argue. I was happy for the drive to the station to pass in silence and the journey started as I had hoped. I was on the verge of falling asleep when Kate felt the need to make conversation.

'Did you have a nice time?'

'Yes thanks, it was great. You guys are great hosts.'

There was a few minutes silence when Kate asked, 'Stu, do you ever regret splitting up?'

It is strange how people find pleasure in the suffering of others. I knew she wanted to hear how sad I was, how much I wanted her back and, although the truth was more complicated than I could explain in the 'one sentence' explanations I knew Kate was after, I obliged.

'Yes, I do. I think she was the only one I ever loved. She was exciting and comfortable at the same time. You know Kate, I do miss her.'

'I believe you Stu. I think people make mistakes and are too scared to go back to the way things were.'

'What about you, Kate. Have you found what you were looking for, your dream?'

There was a silence. It had started raining. The windscreen wipers squeaked as they struggled to find enough water to allow them to do their job comfortably. She didn't reply and I didn't press her. We didn't say much for the rest of the journey. I was tired and glad of the break in conversation. She parked the car and came out to see me on to the train even though I told her it wasn't necessary. The train was already at the platform waiting to start the journey. I said good-bye and kissed Kate on the cheeks.

'It was nice having you over,' said Kate, 'I'm really glad Basil has friends like you.'

'Thanks for the invitation.'

'You must come again, soon.'

'I will.'

Kate stayed on the platform until the train left the station. I waved good-bye and saw her disappear in the distance.

When I got home I noticed an SMS I had missed while on the train. It was from Kate. She hoped I had got home alright. I replied.

It had been a nice day spent with them. I was sated and had drunk enough to allow me to fall asleep without much difficulty in front of the television.

♩♩♩

It was a few days later that I got an email.

'Hi, it's me. Hope you're keeping well. We had a nice time. Basil says we must have you over soon. I'm glad I have a friend like you. I'm sorry I didn't answer your question; the one about my dreams. I have so many but I can't put them into words. You asked me twice and I wanted to answer, but I couldn't, maybe next time. I think I need some time to think. Anyway have a good evening. Kate.'

It was the following weekend that I got an SMS from her. She said she was in town and wondered whether I had time to meet up. I had to give the car in for an MOT which needed a few hours so I agreed to meet up with her for a coffee. She gave me an address which wasn't hard to find. She'd been waiting for about twenty minutes. I noticed the shopping bags; H&M, Zara and Intimissimi.

'Hi, I'm sorry I'm late.'

'That's alright.'

'How are you?'

'Fine,' she smiled.

I was going to give her a hello kiss but it didn't feel right so I took a seat across from her.

It was only as I sat down that, for a moment, I wondered what I was doing there and why I hadn't thought of that earlier. Was I meeting a friend's wife, a friend of mine...or was there something else that I didn't want to name?

She looked prettier than I remembered. Her face, lightly made-up, revealed freckles normally associated with adolescence. Perhaps it was the uncertainty in the way she carried herself.

I realised neither of us said anything since we met and I thought of something to say. She smiled as if she heard what I was thinking. I smiled too.

'So, have you come to tell me about your dreams?'

'Well, yes I suppose that is why I wanted to see you. I almost changed my mind while I was waiting for you because I couldn't decide how I would begin.'

I waited for her to continue. The pause allowed the waiter to take our order and return with mugs of hot water and tea bags. It was a long pause without conversation in which we became strangers sharing a table. As soon as the waiter left us she began to speak.

'Stu, I don't know why I'm here. I hope you don't mind me saying so. I just wanted to see you. Ever since you left I have been trying to understand why you look as if you are merely existing rather than living. Do you understand what I mean?'

'Don't bother trying to work me out.' I said, 'I'm not that complicated.'

'But you are! You're a friend and one should care about what friends are feeling. I mean you care about me otherwise you wouldn't have asked me that question. You don't ask any old person what their dreams are. Do you?'

I was confused by the question.

'Look Kate, just tell me what's troubling you.'

She looked away, hesitated and started speaking as if she were speaking to an imaginary person standing on the other side of the shop window.

'I've been married for two years. It was a wonderful wedding. I thought I was so much in love with him. He seemed so strong, so determined, someone you could depend on and I was so happy when he proposed to me. I really was. I told all my friends, my family, everyone how lucky I was.'

She paused, taking a sip of tea as if she needed to think about something.

'But, when the time came, the day of the wedding, I had to drag myself through it. When leaving for the airport to go on our honeymoon I started crying inconsolably as soon as we got into the limousine. Basil said it was just nerves. He said I would get over it. I didn't. I was numb all through the honeymoon. Basil was disappointed. He threw a tantrum once or twice, but nothing serious. When you were over last time you said 'something happens and you just don't feel the same.' Remember? Well, that's what happened.'

The last thing I wanted to be was a marriage guidance counsellor, especially with my record. It was, however, as she was speaking that it came to me why I was there. I didn't come to see her just because I was a friend, I found her attractive. Basil faded very much into the background. I was attracted to her. There was no other reason.

Kate stopped talking, looked at me and smiled with the sad eyes that remind you of someone in mourning.

I looked at my watch and saw it was already three o'clock. The garage said the car would be ready for four. The garage shut at six and, with an hour back on the tube, I had about an hour free.

'Look Kate, how are you getting home? I've got to pick the car up at four so why don't you come with me and I'll drive you home.'

I paid the bill, helped her with the bags and we left.

I only realised later that evening running through what had happened that she hadn't said a word. She hadn't either questioned or agreed with my suggestion. It was as if she'd been in a daze. We didn't speak much all the way home. In fact, we hardly acknowledged that we were together.

When we got to my flat I opened the door, walked in, placed the bags on the floor, and turned to see her standing in the doorway. She moved towards me and kissed me. It wasn't a passionate kiss, but gentle, as if to acknowledge an almost inevitability about what was happening.

We made love as gently as the kiss. There was hardly any passion involved. Afterwards, lying beside me with her face partly hidden by her hair, I was thinking about something to say. She noticed and before I could say anything she touched my lips with her fingers to hush me. I caressed her moist face and, in that moment, remembered what love had felt like all those years ago.

I drove her to the train station. There were no words of good-bye. She quietly got out of the car and left. She didn't look back. I watched her go into the station and enjoyed looking at the woman I had not long ago only felt and not seen.

$$\mathcal{JV}$$

Stories like this usually end with the break-up of a friendship, the end of an affair or divorce.

I didn't know what to think when Basil rang me a few weeks later and invited me to dinner. I thanked him, but said I was feeling unwell.

'Yes, well, you do sound strange. Oh come on, don't be such a sop! Kate wants to see you too. Here, she wants to speak with you.'

'Hi Stu, how are you?'

I heard him in shouting in the background, 'tell him he's just being a wimp!'

'Did you hear that? We really would love to see you. You are the only one of Basil's friends that I really like. Do come.'

I didn't connect the two people I knew by the name of Kate. This one sounded like the wife of my friend, not the accidental lover I'd met a few weeks earlier.

I went down. I didn't feel uncomfortable while I was there and Kate gave me no reason to think that she did either. She looked very different; more settled, happily playing the housewife trying to please.

There are moments when I wonder whether anything really happened. I tried to notice any traces of the girl I'd met that Saturday afternoon but couldn't.

You see, I told you this wasn't going to be a love story and, I suppose, in a way it isn't. But...I think love's got something to do with it, hasn't it?

*   *   *

Michael

J

The cathartic exercise started at two in the morning. It was just another sleepless night for Michael. Not something that he ever got used to despite having been through similar nights before, but this time there was a throbbing pain. It had started at the back of the neck and worked its way up to the back of the head, probably another migraine again.

The night was silent except for the occasional car passing by, carrying passengers from one sleepless venue to the next.

He sat by the window of his fifth floor apartment looking out at the building across the road. There were still a few lights shining through curtains that discretely hid the nocturnal lives led by others. He didn't need to draw the curtains. There was nothing to hide. He had memories that hid behind eyes wide open barely covered by eye lids which were also wide awake. He kept them secret in daylight hours under cover of the routine of everyday life, but now they came back as mixed up as his understanding of life. He sometimes thought of people who found it hard to remember and the torture they felt they were going through. If only he could explain to them how much better off they were.

'So tell me,' he asked himself, 'who do you think you are?'

The question was first posed in innocent cleverness by a colleague of average intelligence. I don't know whether she really understood the magnitude of the effect it had on him. He wanted to answer, but as he tried to form words in reply, he realised that he didn't have anything convincing to say. It was an unfair question; one of those that no single answer could be enough. He tried to remind himself of the circumstances in which the question had been posed, but she didn't give him a chance. She smiled as he ran out of time.

'Who do you think I am?' he asked, hoping she wouldn't notice the deflection.

She smiled in answer to his question leaving him to think about the answer he could have given.

He couldn't sleep. He had tried for over two hours. When he was younger he thought it was 'cool' to be known as an insomniac. It made him feel special. It brought him notoriety.

'You just can't sleep can you? I wish I had the same problem. There are so many more things that I would be able to do.'

Michael hated them all. All those clever people that tried to give the impression they understood.

'You know, I could sleep but I don't want to. If you were here with me I would fall asleep.'

He was trying to understand why he couldn't sleep, making up stories.

'What's your name?'

He knew her name. It was, but no he wouldn't say it. He promised he would never say that name out aloud. That was a nice game. He

147

tried to break his promise, say it quietly, but then panicked because he couldn't remember it.

'Is that you again? Have you come back to me? Will you open the door once more and say who you are?

That is not how it happened. His memories were playing games.

'Now you see me, now you don't. Ha ha ha! Idiot! You don't know who I am!'

A car drove past. One of its headlights wasn't working. It blinked as it drove past. Michael could have remembered more than just the name if he wanted to, but he had shut out the memories. It was only in his loneliness that they struggled to break free. He indulged in self pity for a moment, for reassurance. The darkness of the night sky helped. There were no stars, and the moon hid behind dark still clouds making faces at him.

Another car drove past. The headlights were switched to beam. The night air was cool. Summer had arrived too soon and the battle of the seasons had not yet been won. The last gasp of winter had killed the early spring flowers with an unexpected frost. Other things were dying too.

Another car drove past. Quicker than the last, it was obviously going somewhere.

'Do you really care, or are you just asking me questions because you think you will impress me with your cleverness?'

There wasn't an answer. That's what did to you at two in the morning; posed questions and made up answers. Michael was clever. If he hadn't been tired, he would have replied.

'You know, I like you. In fact I think I'm in love with you. No, I know that I am. I am, aren't I? I think of you all the time. That must be love mustn't it?'

There it was again. A lifetime of indulgence had not taught Michael any lessons. He was still burdened by the imagination he had as a child. The trouble was he had too much time on his hands. Insomniacs always do.

'Don't you get tired?'

'Yes, I do. I am. Help me.'

It was hopeless. He knew it would continue until the bed sheets shaped into the mess of the loveless exercise he remembered.

'I like Egon Schiele.'

Michael remembered who had said that before. There was somebody. He knew who it was, but struggled to uncover the face or find a name that would fit. It sounded different then. His answer had been the same, but somehow it was gentle this time. There was an innocence in the way she said she liked Schiele. None of the vulgar eroticism he remembered.

'Lucien Freud was the better artist. You could smell the flesh in Freud's work.'

'No, I think Schiele was more honest, adolescent honesty. Like puppy love.'

'No, yes, maybe, I don't care.'

'That's the problem.'

'Why can't I forget you?'

'Because you don't want to.'

Michael had nothing better to do. That was the problem, not Schiele. He had time. He had already made of life what he believed he could. There was not much more to do. No more causes to fight. Michael wondered whether

Salman Rushdie had used notoriety as a means to give him some purpose. Who would ever have heard of him if it hadn't been for the controversies? Police protection didn't cost him anything. Freedom was something he'd given up for something more; a reason to go on living. Michael was no Salman Rushdie.

'You know I've always been a rebel.'

'Really,' she smiled, 'and tell me what have you done that's been so rebellious?' Have you ever taken drugs?'

'Well, no. I nearly did, once. I had friends who did.'

'Do you have any piercings?' she laughed.

'No, but that's a good idea, maybe an earring?'

'Oh yes, that would be very rebellious.'

He wanted to grab hold of her and kiss that smile away.

'Alright, what about a tattoo?'

It was a last ditched attempt at trying to impress, but he knew he had lost it.

'I could get a tattoo, a dragon that should have faded quietly away but remains as a reminder of youthful rebellion, and then I'd be just like you!' but she wasn't listening.

Another car drove past. No respect for speed cameras this time. That person definitely knew where he wanted to get to!

It was getting late. Morning would be upon him and then he would join colleagues refreshed from a good night's sleep. He would be numb so that all he would do would be to smile. Only his body would be tired. His mind would surface from the night, agile enough to understand the decisions he was incapable of making.

Enough, Michael decided to go to bed. Sleep would come later if he was lucky. He needed an incentive. He decided that the best thing to her being there was to get into bed and think of something pleasant, perhaps even dream of her. He had never liked blondes, but then that was in the past. He needed a name. He thought for a minute and then as the next car drove past it threw him a thought. It must be Sarah. Sarah, with her soft skin covering a body that had already tried the experiences that excite youth and dissolve with age into incidental memory. It was definitely her, a wild one tamed by misfortune. There was no pity for her because she was like all the others he had met. Each had a story which when repeated over the first, or was it the second drink of the second date, in the sincere belief that it was an original, but like most of the things that happened to him, there was nothing new.

'Sarah, it must be you.'

Sarah was special. She was a new love. The first new love.

JJ

I saw you in the corridor. I saw you by the photo-copier that stood against the wall. I recognised you by the way your hair fell over your shoulders. You didn't notice me. I walked passed and inhaled. There was no fragrance.

I said hello and you replied. I didn't hear the words, but I saw your smile. I didn't know

151

your name, but decided it must be Sarah, and it was. That was what it was like before we met, before we shared confidences. I thought long and hard about how it would start. Our acquaintance, I mean. You were so close to me and yet the barriers we created offered no opportunity.

I saw you every day and thought that would be enough. I could say a word a day to you and that would be enough. I could imagine the rest. After all isn't that what dreams are made of; imagination.

There was something different about you. There always is. Every time I indulge in the fantasy of falling in love there is a large dose of imagination. You were different to the rest. You always had to be. If you weren't, it wouldn't matter because I would imagine you different. I never compared you to the rest because I could make you different.

I met you in the park that afternoon. The sky looked pale in the sunshine and you sat in the shade reading a book. I waited for you to realise I was there. It was easy. You looked up and smiled. I walked up to you and asked you what book you were reading. I was surprised.

I asked if I could join you and you said yes. I did. The grass was damp. I asked why you liked the book you were reading and you gave me a lecture on the brilliance of the authors' insight in the Middle East conflict. I thought it was a strange book for a Jew, but I didn't say anything to you.

I imagined you as an intellectual but you weren't. I imagined what you might think if I told you that you were trying too hard and that life was not really that complicated, but I knew you wouldn't understand. Everyone has the right to suffer. That was something I learned a long time ago and I had to allow you the freedom to suffer. It was different for me. I had learned to suffer at the hands of others. Jesus had died for my sins and now it was my turn to die for you. We all had to die. The crucifixion was no easier at the age of thirty-three. You had reached the age when something inside you would die too and I would have to watch it happen. That is what love is.

We walked down a hill. It was dark. I bought a hand full of bubble gum called 'Love is.' You smiled as you took them and ate one. I asked whether you would let me have one. You said I could have the one you were chewing. I stole half as we kissed. It still tastes of you. It was a nice dream Sarah. We were children then and now we aren't. Now you're pregnant and starting life as a one parent family. Your hair is dirty now and so are your clothes. Now I will leave you because you don't want pity. You vomit and call it morning sickness. It smells like vomit no matter what you call it. Call it love.

I don't like this dream. It started nicely, but it's not what I want, so I change it.

We are walking hand in hand through gardens. We are in love. It's our day off and we are making the most of it. I like your dress. It's a nice summer dress that reveals your form, discreet enough for me to know what it hides. They're sweet, those feelings you excite in me. Your body is soft and pale, and those enticing shadows make me want to caress you. You slip off your sandals and give me your feet to rub. My hands smell of the fresh grass that stained your feet. Your hair falls across your face and you carelessly wave it back around your ears. I could have told you that your hair wouldn't stay in place. Later, you realise it too and wind it into a bun revealing a neck stained with light freckles.

Yes, I remember, that's how it was. It's not a dream anymore. It's become a memory. You had smudged your lipstick on the corner of your mouth, but I didn't say anything. I knew if I had you would have spent the next ten minutes getting it right and, I didn't want you stealing ten precious minutes from me.

We lay back on the grass and watched the clouds. I didn't want to know this wouldn't last forever. You got up and brushed the back of your dress. I watched. You saw me and did it again. You asked me whether everything was all right. I gave you a 'thank you' kiss. I held your hand as we walked through the gardens. I was in love.

I reached out to hold you again but you weren't there. I awoke to the emptiness of the night. I pulled your pillow towards me trying to smell your fragrance, but there was nothing, and then I remembered we were in the past. You had not yet become mine. I was in love again. I tried to think how much I loved you, but your absence interfered. You were not there. I thought of how you would come to me the first time, and I, unsure of how I would begin if it was me you relied on. I thought we could kiss until instinct dissolved our shyness. The innocence was sweet. We know nothing lasts forever, but at that moment it wouldn't matter. You would tell me how wonderful it was while I would say a quiet prayer to the God of all the worlds, 'Almighty God, I believe. There is none other than the one and only, and in your mercy I lay open my hope, my wish, my desperate desire for eternity,' and then I would wait, listening hard for his answer in the stillness of the night. I would smile as you snore. You warned me you do but I didn't think it would sound like this. A sound coming from the sleeping animal inside you which, like the feet of a peacock, seemed out of place. Your head would rest on my chest and your saliva drip to create a pool that I would wait to wipe away when you wouldn't notice me do so. I drift into the calm my tired body creates and hear the trees rustle in the wind outside my window. It is still my window, not ours; you aren't here. It is still all a dream, all except the prayer. It starts to rain. I hear its irregular rhythm and wonder where you are now.

'Hello, is that you?'

'Hello.'

I don't know what to say except that I want the conversation to last forever.

'Do you like apples?'

You laugh. You understand what is happening. I struggle to think of what to say and then there's a throbbing in my head. It comes and goes, and then comes back again. It sounds like the echo of my heart, but still hurts.

'Do you love me?'

No, I don't like this dream either. I look at the clock on the wall and concentrate through the darkness until I see the time. Half past four. I have three hours to go. I don't know what to do. I get up and walk over to Michael.

JJJ

He's still sitting there quietly staring at the wall in front of him. He still can't sleep. He's numb. I can't help him. I thought sleep would do him good but he doesn't want to sleep. He's still looking for something to hold on to.

'Do you love me?'

He looks for answers in the static created by a myriad of thoughts that infuse his mind.

'You know I love you, but do you love me?'

'And what if I say 'yes', will it make it alright.'

He knows it won't.

'You're right. It is a stupid question. It doesn't mean anything.'

'Do you like asking questions that don't have answers?'

The pain starts again. Maybe he's been thinking too much. Maybe he needs a rest. It's a throbbing pain. Yes, he needs to get some rest. He has to go to work tomorrow.

Michael gets up and staggers to bed. He lies in bed listening to the rain. All he wants is an answer to a simple question. He doesn't realise there are no answers, just conversations that scramble around trying to convey meaning, trying to make sense.

'I think I'm tired.'

'Yes, I think you should go to sleep.'

'I wish you were by my side.'

She laughs. She always laughs. He likes the sound of her laughter.

'Well, maybe I will one day. You never know.'

He smiles.

'Well you're right,' he answers, 'one day maybe you will and then I'll know.'

He can't remember whether she ever was by his side. He thinks she must have been because he knows she isn't there now. They come back to him, those memories, in the guise of a slow piercing pain inside his head.

Michael's tired. He should sleep. He shuts his eyes following the blood vessels to the source of the pain inside his head. He knew it was there before the doctors told him. They were sorry. He was too.

Another car drives past. No headlights this time. It's morning. It drives past quietly so as to not wake the neighbours. They need to go to work. They will find out later.

A tear slips out of the corner of his eye and drips on to the pillow.

'Are you crying?'

There is no answer. Michael lies silent in the darkness, bloated, still as death. Death has a fragrance. It smells like when you used to fart in bed.

'I'm sorry Michael.'

There won't be a reply.

There were no sirens. It was too late to make a fuss. The ambulance came quietly to take his memories away.

*   *   *

157

Eve

I troubles me why, when everything falls into place as part of a routine that we come to rely on, we should think about what it might have been like if things had been different. But we do. In idle moments of contentment we think about the 'what ifs?' Not necessarily with regret or sadness, just a pleasant way to pass the time.

The first time I met Eve was when she was going out with Kevin. Kevin was an old friend from school with whom I had lost touch shortly after starting university. We had been good friends, especially in the last two years at school and, although we swore university wouldn't make any difference to our friendship, I think we underestimated the excitement of living away from home. We hoped that we would be together after school and applied to the same university. There was little difference in our 'A' level grades, but fate intervened, and we ended up going to universities at different ends of the country; me to Exeter and Kevin to Lancaster. While we met up on holidays in the first year it seems plain in hindsight that our first summer holiday was the beginning of our friendship moving on from adolescent attachment to the longevity of acquaintance.

After finishing university I moved back to London. Kevin decided he liked the north and found a job in Manchester. Our parents continued to live in the same terraced houses we grew up in continuing the friendship between them that started with our very first 'parent/teacher' meeting at secondary school.

Kevin and I went to an all boys' school and Eve went to a girls' school.

Kevin met Eve in a newsagents; a shop in those days that was able to live off selling newspapers, some sweets and a little stationary. We were seventeen and in our second year of 'A' levels and Eve, a year younger, getting ready to start her 'A' levels. She had gone to get some cigarettes for her father as had Kevin, a Sunday newspaper.

Those were in the days when children rebelled a little later than they do now; the good old days of smoking at petrol stations, growing pot in window boxes outside bedroom windows on the pretext of a science project if discovered by nosey parents and, the innocence of elderly neighbours who forever treated us like children. Kevin had queued up behind Eve and, not realising that someone was standing close behind her, she had been embarrassed bumping into him. I'm sure, knowing Kevin that he was more embarrassed by it than Eve. After that first meeting he talked about Eve all the time.

Kevin was helping his mum with some shopping a couple of weeks later when he saw her again. She was doing much the same with her mother and he saw her first. She had just turned a corner into the dairy section of Tesco's. He left his mum at the meat counter debating with the butcher about what to get and raced round before his mum had time to notice he'd disappeared. He got back to his mum and almost got a clout for disappearing like that, but it was worth it because he got her name. It wasn't a phone number, but he was very pleased with himself.

The following Sunday while his father was smoking his pipe over the Sunday paper and his mother was washing the dishes left after lunch, Kevin picked up the telephone directory to look up Eve's number. He told me later how he had struggled to find her as the list of Patersons was almost a page long. He finally got through and rang to tell me that they had arranged to meet at McDonalds. He told me that I had to come along, in fact almost begged me.

Eve was surprised to see me and, while Kevin's bravado increased by having me there, her shyness betrayed the innocence of someone not accustomed to new relationships. It was easy for me because, although green with envy, I was able to enjoy the company of a girl with whom I could relax.

The relationship continued throughout the summer and, by the winter, both sets of parents were happy to allow Kevin to bring Eve over to listen to records in his bedroom where they practiced the art of kissing learned from friends with more imagination than experience.

I used to go over and watch their antics as I hid behind LP covers of T Rex or Iron Maiden which we played as loudly as we could without his parents shouting at us to keep the noise down. Spring came, and with exams to worry about after disastrous mocks, I left them to it.

It was Eve, waiting for 'A' level results the following summer, when we both came back home from university that we met again. A year at university had changed us both and that was perhaps Eve's disappointment. Kevin had moved on in terms of relationships and I, with energy spent trying an intellectual angle to impress the opposite sex was still in the infancy of sexual awareness. It was perhaps Kevin's taunting that made meeting him less pleasant for me as well as my virgin righteousness that disgusted me at the way he treated Eve.

We promised to meet up during the Christmas break but Kevin didn't come down. I saw Eve in the market that Christmas and that is how it all started.

'Hi Eve.'

'Hi Harry.'

'How's Uni?'

'OK.'

'Haven't seen Kevin. I heard he isn't coming down for Christmas.'

'Yeh fucked off, the bastard!'

It was a stronger reaction than I expected, especially as Kevin was still my friend. She must have noticed me wince.

'So, what about you? Still trying to impress girls with intellectual crap or have you decided to turn gay?'

I recovered enough not to reply. I gave her a neutral smile which I think must have made her realise that she had gone a little too far.

'So what you are you doing here?' she said.

'Mum asked me to get some veggies, what about you?'

'Yeh, me too.

I'd borrowed Dad's car and gave her a lift home.

'Thanks Harry. By the way I didn't mean to be a shit earlier.'

'No worries. See you around.'

Eve rang me on Christmas day to wish me a Merry Christmas. Everyone was over; Uncles Joe and Lawrence, Aunties Edith and Jackie and Cousin Helen. Gramps was over too. Uncle Joe answered the phone and shouted over the noise, 'Harry, your girlfriend's on the phone.' I was embarrassed and rushed over to take the receiver from him.

I could tell she'd heard Uncle Joe by the sheepish way in which she said 'hello'.

'Oh, hi.' Sorry about that,' I whispered. The conversation had died down in the sitting room and I was sure everyone was eaves dropping.

'Yes, sorry, I feel as if I'm interrupting. I just thought I'd wish you a Merry Christmas.'

'Yes, thanks, Merry Christmas.'

'I didn't have your address otherwise I'd have sent you a card.'

'Don't worry.'

There was a pause in the conversation.

'OK, I'll see you around.'

'Eve.'

'Yes.'

'Do you wanna meet up?' I said nervously.

'Yes, maybe,'

I heard that to mean 'yes' and took her phone number.

After the call I went back to the sitting room wading through the mess to grab myself another beer.

'So, why didn't you invite your girlfriend round?' asked Uncle Joe.

'What's this about a girlfriend?' asked Mum.

'I, I haven't got a girlfriend,' I stammered. I must have turned beetroot because they all laughed.

'Yeh, well make sure it's safe sex and all that,' said Uncle Joe. 'You know what's going around,' he continued with a smirk.

I ignored the questions and everyone soon lost interest except Mum. She reserved her questions for the privacy of her son's bedroom later that evening. I didn't want to, but knowing she wouldn't give up, I decided to tell her about Eve.

'It's no-one Mum. Just someone I met, a friend from an old crowd that I used to hang out with when I was at school. I haven't seen her for a while and met her in the street the other day.' It was an effort to get it all out in one go, but I was glad I made it!

'Is she nice?'

'Sort of.'

'What's her name?'

'Eve.'

'That's a nice name. Well, you'll know when the time is right to introduce us, won't you.'

'Yes Mum.'

And that was that. She had enough information to leave me alone for the moment.

I rang Eve the next day. Boxing Day is usually dull when we are all trying to recover from over-eating and hangovers that don't allow a good night's sleep.

'Hi, Harry. Sorry about yesterday. Look I've gotta go, can we speak when I get back. I'll give you a ring,' and she rang off.

I felt a bit odd holding a phone with no-one at the other end and replaced the receiver as soon as I realised what I was doing. It was a delayed reaction that maybe you'll understand...a strange notion of something having happened but not quite knowing what.

She didn't ring. I waited, but not to the exclusion of doing other things. The kind of waiting that pops up as an unexpected reminder in the middle of doing ordinary things like helping Mum clear away the table, or putting out the rubbish, but all the time half listening to hear whether the imaginary ring of the telephone could be real.

I remembered her again as I lay in bed that evening, annoyed at myself for having telephoned her. She wasn't that great. Just a girl I knew. The girls at university were ok but this was different. She was someone I knew. Kevin's ex, that was all. She was just a friend I told myself, nothing more than that.

I seemed to be only one down from University. The days between Christmas and New Year were the most boring. Most of my old friends had disappeared and my new friends were far away.

She was still sleeping when I rang her the next day. He mother had woken her up. She hadn't told me Eve was asleep.

'Hello.'

'Hi.'

I could tell from her voice that the reality of the living world was slowly dawning on her.

'Did I wake you?'

'No, that's alright. What time is it?'

'Eleven.'

I imagined her in bed wearing a T-shirt and knickers. White, like the ones I'd seen her wearing as Kevin and Eve had rolled around on his bed.

'Shall I ring back?'

'No, when are you going back to University?'

'Next Sunday.'

'You?'

'Sunday too.'

'Do you want to meet up for a drink sometime?'

'OK, could meet up tonight if you want.'

I felt a flutter of excitement having achieved something I had not expected. We agreed where and when and she rang off.

I borrowed Dad's car. He was good about that. Unlike my friends, my parents didn't give me much to complain about. It meant that I wouldn't be able to have more than one drink, but I decided having the car was worth it.

I picked her up at eight outside her house. I was about to get out of the car when she came out of her front door. She's punctual, I thought.

We didn't go for a drink. Instead we went to a fish n chip place she liked.

'You smelt nice when you got in the car and now you're gonna smell like fish n chips!'

'Yeh, you too, smelly!'

We laughed. It was fun. We talked about Uni, the friends we'd made, the music she liked.

She had moved on to David Bowie and Bryan Ferry. We had both mellowed.

We stank of fish n chips when we got back into the car and lit cigarettes to get rid of the smell.

It was still only half past nine so we took a drive to Wandsworth Common. I asked her whether she wanted to go for a walk, but she said it was too cold and couldn't we just stay in the car. That was fine by me. I parked the car and was wondering whether she was expecting me to make a move when she interrupted.

'So, what's it like going out with your friend's girlfriend?'

The question threw me and I struggled to find something to say. She laughed at my discomfort and, for a moment, I regretted being with her.

'It's OK, Harry. We've broken up. Why don't you impress me with something?'

'Look, Eve. I'm sorry I just thought it might be nice seeing you.'

'Aw, Harry got the hump?'

'OK, let's go,' I said, reaching for the car keys when she held my arm to stop me.

'I'm sorry, God you are the sensitive type! So, tell me, you got a girlfriend?'

'No, not really.'

'You've been at Uni for over a year.'

'Yeh, well. Having a girlfriend's different to getting laid.'

I knew a few girls, but none I liked enough to call my girlfriend and especially not while I was with Eve.

'So, you want me to be your girlfriend?'

'I don't know,' I said not really sure what answer she expected.

'Well, you gotta try to snog me if you want to have a chance. Being a gentleman and all that shit is fine, but it's not going to get you anywhere.'

I stopped thinking and kissed her. We spent the best part of half an hour kissing. She was obviously better at it than I was and I was surprised with excitement as I felt her tongue exploring my mouth. Her saliva tasted sweet. I stroked her hair, felt her ears and moved into as much of an embrace as the front seats of the car would allow. I felt the urge to do more than just kiss but hadn't come prepared.

As I drove her home I noticed that the little intimacy we had enjoyed had made her pensive. I imagined us both thinking about what had happened. It was when we stopped outside her house that she turned to me. When I noticed she'd been crying, I panicked.

'I'm sorry,' I said, with a mixture of fear and genuine concern; fear because I wondered what her parents might think as she walked into the house obviously having been crying, and concern because I didn't know what I was guilty of.

'Harry, I still think of him. I don't know why he dumped me. He said he wouldn't and nothing I let him do was enough to keep him. I wanted to meet you because it was as close as I could get to him.'

I was lost for words. The fear evaporated and the concern turned to anger. I felt used. After what had happened in the park I thought we had something. I liked her. I decided I had liked her from the very first day we met in McDonalds. I envied Kevin and was glad he hadn't come down for Christmas. I never thought it could happen but it did. I didn't go looking for her like Kevin did. She just appeared. If I hadn't met her at the market we would have gone our separate ways, maybe never met up again, but the fact that we had meant something. And now this!

'Harry, do you hate me?'

'Yes, but it's OK. I'll see you around,' I said in cue for her to get out of the car. She hesitated to give me a chance to change my mind. I remember hearing her say sorry as she left the car.

I drove home trying to forget I'd made a fool of myself.

Eve rang me that evening, but I told Mum to say I'd ring back. I didn't.

She rang again once before I left for University, but I didn't take the call. We didn't meet again.

Now, with more time to spend with memories, I wonder about the 'what ifs'. Insignificant as it all was, only made important by the adolescence that consumed us at the time, I think of Eve and our first kiss. I wonder what it would've been like if it had been Eve lying here beside me.

*　　　*　　　*

The Rose

J

I know there's nothing like love at first sight. I'm not stupid. Nourished by failed relationships in which I considered love and sex to be equal partners I find ways to ease the pain of being alone. Not old enough to content myself with lurid fantasies I hover in the expectation that something enduring could still be waiting for me. And then, suddenly, out of the blue, it happens! Without any pre-planned adventure that could take the credit for what might be, it happens! Bored with uninspiring television dinners eaten out of necessity, my senses, which ones exactly I can't remember, are thrown into turmoil.

Of course, it's a girl or boy, that stop me dead in my tracks and, as famously as the desperate passion that rends the heart in Nabokov's famous diatribe; Lolita, I decide I've found what I am looking for. There is no doubt.

I have been sitting in this bar drinking tonic water that only adds to the disappointment of trying to finish the five hundred words I need to do tonight to avoid the editor finally giving me up as unreliable and, stuck at about three hundred with nothing more to say, I waste my time on watching middle-aged patrons indulge themselves in the attention of waiters who serve. The European ten percent tip paid with exaggerated generosity absolves them just in case there is a God or another guest watching, ready to pass judgement.

There is nothing inspiring in what I see as I take another sip of the tasteless penance staring at my laptop that is as depressed as I am.

'Would you like anything else, Sir?'

I look up, half ignoring the image of the waitress in front of me, smile a practiced indifferent smile to shoo her away whispering 'no thanks,' and, just as she's about to turn, I notice her.

No description of her would do her justice. I could say that she was about five feet five, blonde, hair tied back in a pony tail with a black ribbon keeping it all in place. I could tell you that she was slight, quiet, with shadowed sleeplessness that could not lie. She had eyes that smiled with lips in matt finished red lip gloss that have never known lipstick. Her open shirt revealed a touch of perspiration and everything else left to imagination. And legs, as she turned and walked away after hearing my involuntary 'no thank you,' moved with a weariness that only a sadist would find endearing.

Nothing I have told you about her could tell you what I saw in those first few seconds it took to see what I've just described. You must, I regret, be left looking at a photograph seen using the crutches of intellect. Deprived of fragrances that mingled in the air or sound of silent steps, strands of hair dancing off shoulders, or the eloquent etiquette of fingers holding cups and saucers with grace beyond the sound of mortal composition, like the rustle of leaves in trees, or the drizzle of rain that indulge fantasies born of more than mere physical desire. All this I can tell you and yet, I cannot tell you all that I saw.

'No thanks,' I said, and she turned and left, rejected, but it was I who was the one rejected! By myself! I called her back, but the embarrassment of those who might hear made me call her too softly and, by the time I had heard the inadequacy of my voice, it was too late. She had gone. Gone too far to hear me call and I, too intimidated by the guilt of what I'd seen, couldn't call her again.

I distracted myself with the words I'd written and, annoyed at the inadequacy of my talent, stared accusingly at the screen. I had to finish the piece. Five hundred words to make something of a non-event, a lie that others would read in the hope of arousing enough excitement for the reader to form an opinion that could be used in idle conversation.

In anger I put a space between the last paragraph and the rest of the text, made up a story describing a scene that could have taken place in the context of the piece. The anger was enough to last the two hundred words I needed and, closing the piece with words I'd thought of before I started writing it, I saved it as 'final'. I didn't want to read it again for fear of disappointment so e mailed the story to the editor.

I finished my drink and waited for the waitress to come back, but she stayed away sending a colleague to try his luck where she had failed.

'No thank you, just the bill, please.'

I signed the bill to my room and went up to bed. The next day I would leave this city unless I could find a reason to stay.

The next morning I awoke early for breakfast. There were not many people in the dining room and I found a table, switched on my computer to see whether I had received any e mails. I expected the editor to be angry with me for the quality of the piece I'd sent in. His e mail was waiting for me.

'Thanks. Got it, if there is so much brewing stay a couple of days longer,' he wrote in the style of a telegram that e mail correspondence had gone back to. I was surprised enough to look again at what I had sent him and smiled to myself with the mischievousness that 'Our Man in Havana' might have felt had he not been so desperate.

I was quietly thinking to myself when I heard a voice.

'Would you like some coffee?'

I looked up and saw her again. Her practised smile hid the tiredness of her eyes. This time I said 'Yes, please,' louder than I intended that made her jump. I was too delighted by the chance meeting I believed this to be and didn't want to make the same mistake I'd made the night before. She poured and the smell of coffee, infused with her early morning washed freshness, made me dizzy.

'I didn't think I'd see you again,' I said. Her smile continued. I filled the sound of pouring coffee with words, 'I saw you last night. I thought you might have the morning off.'

'No, Sir. Tomorrow is my day off.'

'And what do you do on your day off?'

172

She looked at me with those eyes that were at once innocent and knowing.

'Would you like some milk?'

'No, thank you.'

She turned and walked away. I felt like a fool, but not embarrassed. I laughed at my bravado of asking what she did on her day off. I ignored the failure of not finding out and, instead, enjoyed the pleasure of watching her move between the few occupied tables carrying the jugs of coffee and milk. There was nothing special in the way she moved, nothing practiced, just the matter of factness of the way we all go about our work. The smile fixed, I imagined, after countless innocent trials in front of a mirror that hid her childlike nervousness of applying herself in a grown up world.

I couldn't guess how old she was but that didn't matter. There was nothing obscene in my thoughts, but nothing noble either. It was a simple matter of wanting to be with her, not in her arms, not to taste those lips, not to float in the gentle sound waves of her voice; simply to be with her. I didn't know what that meant and didn't want to try to understand what that meant either. Was it love, infatuation, or some hopelessness that hides in a dark corner of our souls and, when prodded accidentally in a rare moment of ennui, erupts to consume us? I was a slave, mesmerized by the hypnotic effect of everything I'd experienced until that moment in my life.

She returned soon after leaving but this time with a knowing smile. She knew, I was sure, and I was glad because now I was no longer in control. Destiny had taken over.

She didn't ask before she poured the coffee and, this time, added milk. As she did so, her eyes stared into mine as if daring me to flirt with her again. Lost for words I stared back pleading with her to stop the torment.

'Anything else, Sir,' she said emphasising the 'Sir' as if to make a point.

'Yes,' I said, my bravado having unexpectedly returned, 'can I see you tomorrow?'

'Why?'

'I don't know,' I replied, 'if I could, I'd love to.'

I thought I heard a 'maybe' as she walked away, only this time I noticed a swagger of her hips as if she was doing a victory dance. I thought she might turn back to make sure I was still looking, but I over estimated her confidence.

I drank my coffee surveying the tables around me that had been occupied during my trance, trying to establish whether my foolishness had been noticed. I didn't notice anything unusual.

I thought about the rules of the hotel, whether fraternising with guests meant instant dismissal. I imagined an unwelcome sense of power at the thought of compromising the object of my affection. I assumed and, in that assumption, wondered what sort of poverty had deprived her of an education driving her to the sort of work that had no prospect of a career. I felt the desperate need to protect the angel I'd been sent to rescue, but didn't know how. I, a failed writer that struggled with assignments of five hundred words, allowed to stay on only because he'd been inspired by a muse, was hardly someone worthy enough to whisk her away to some golden sanded island deep in some gentle blue ocean, to stay there until my very being would be utterly consumed by her. The intrusion of reality left me disgusted with myself. I walked over to the breakfast buffet bar to see whether there was anything that my gluttony would attract and, before returning to my table, I looked around just in case I might see her again.

I saw her looking at me and this time her smile seemed mocking, but I forgave her unkindness with a smile of my own sincere with disappointment, turned and walked back to my table.

I ate with gluttonous gratitude thinking about the next piece I needed to send to my editor that day, thinking of new exaggerations to inspire me. I looked around again and saw someone occupy the table in front of me. Young, gelled dark hair, a sharp pinstripe suit with the smell of eau de cologne of power and money. A thought occurred to me and I started writing.

The next time I looked up I saw her again. This time with her back to me, leaning over the table pouring coffee and, at that very moment, I felt a surge of energy sparking across my mind. I pulled out a business card and looked for something to write with. I had nothing with me. I looked up and waited to catch her attention. She saw me as she turned and I waved for her to come over to me.

'Yes Sir.'

'May I have a pen, please?'

She put the coffee jugs down; pulled out a pen from a pocket I hadn't noticed.

I crossed out 'Freelance journalist' on the card and wrote. She waited. I then placed the

175

pen on the card and waited for her to take the invitation. She looked at me wondering what she was expected to do and then noticed the card. She picked up the pen and then, like the actress she was, hesitated, picked up the card and left.

♪♪

I felt a sense of excitement through the rest of the day. I turned the pinstripe into a member of the secret service. I turned the woman he had breakfast with into a contact creating an air of suspicion. The demonstrations, brutally put down three months ago, had started a wave of reprisals and there was uneasiness in the air. The five hundred words came easily to me, and I had the presence of mind to ask the editor not to attribute the story to me by name. He wrote back almost immediately asking for more. I said I would write again the next day as I needed to follow up on something. I stayed in my hotel room all morning. I came down for lunch and, after lunch, took a walk in the park just outside the hotel.

There was a chill in the air. Spring was still practicing the opening chords that would inspire flowers to awake from their winter sleep. It was too early to imagine what the future would bring and yet, in the sun, the future was warm. Park benches filled up with the jobless, mostly young and ardent in their search for hope. I could write the next five hundred words or the next thousand simply exaggerating what I saw. I took out a note book and scribbled some notes that I could write up in the evening. I continued my observations until the coldness in the air sent me back to the familiarity of the hotel. Back in my room I sat at my laptop and wrote.

When I had finished, checking to see how many words I'd written, I was pleased with the fluency that writing a lie gave me. I smiled re-reading it with the relish of getting away with slander in this foreign land. I sent it. I knew it was too soon, but didn't worry that I might not be able to take my story to the next chapter. Leaving the computer switched on I decided I deserved a lie down. Exhausted with so much going on I closed my eyes and thought of her, wondering how much longer I'd be allowed to indulge myself.

I wasn't sure she'd come but knowing that she'd taken the card without any prompting, gave me hope. I fell into a dream of walking with her in the park I'd just visited. We talked for the first time. More than who we were, what we did and why, we talked of what we thought and felt.

Too young to realise that life makes no excuses for being unforgiving, she reminded me of how I'd mapped out the years when I was young. I listened, waiting for the right time to say something. It was a long wait because, captivated, I wanted to wait. I didn't want to add this to my memory of practiced stumbling through life. I needed to impress her with intelligence because the language she spoke had no meaning in my world. I had lived with quiet certainty for so long that nothing could change me. I saw her sit on the bench by the artificial lake that had fish eager to be caught by tourists. The rekindling of desire turned me to stone when

177

I thought about the disappointment that life had in store for her.

She talked and I listened, as if all the years of growing up had led her to me and all my years of disappointment had not killed my desire to dream. I saw her as the golden angel painted through the ages, drowned in memories and resurrected in sacred flames of martyrdom. She was all I imagined her to be.

She told me of her dreams; of finding someone to love, of having a house, a car, a family and eternity. She asked me what I wanted. I replied. She laughed when I told her that all I ever wanted was someone like her. I laughed too because I didn't know what else to do.

I must have left the doors to the balcony open. The freshness in the evening air sent a chill to wake me from my dream. I remembered the dream and smiled at its naivety. It was the dream of schoolboys bursting with adolescent enthusiasm and yet, here was I, a man who recorded history to make a living, indulging myself.

I awoke to notice I'd received an email. I thought how pleased the editor would have been to receive the piece, imagining how long I would be left to stay in this forgotten land that had no meaning to anyone, no purpose except to provide entertainment for the indignant.

'Hello, great job. Things are obviously heating up there. Sending Ian. He'll be there tomorrow. Thanks for your great work. He'll take it from here.'

I read it again. I was sure it must be a mistake. Ian was a senior political correspondent who had served in Beirut, Kabul and Baghdad. This was a far cry from the turmoil of such great newsworthy locations and yet, *he* was being sent here; a place where revolutions were only talked about and never happened.

There was too much happening all at once. I had a moment of panic but, with the experience of years, knew how to stay calm. Fate was for the impatient young! I wanted to stay and could. All I needed was an excuse and I had the whole evening to think of one.

I went downstairs to the hotel restaurant and had a light supper. It was already past ten and she would be finishing in an hour or so. I was about to order a coffee when I suddenly had a wonderful idea.

'Do you still serve coffee in the lounge?'

I paid and walked into the lounge with quiet excitement. I was playing a game I had played so many times before; a daisy chain romance of 'would she, wouldn't she?' That spectacular indulgence of age that is as innocent as it is sad, sitting in the confident armchair of smoke filled cigar rooms. I took my seat; mine having used it continuously for three days now, and looked round. I smiled as she came over to serve me.

'Can I get you something?'

It was a wild question full of possibilities all beginning with a one word answer. The hopelessness of so many years smothered the hope of something about to begin. I say begin, but in truth it had more than begun, it was flourishing in the radiance of spring. All thoughts of death were now buried deep in the earth that spring had conquered.

'I'm not sure,' I flirted, trying to hold the vision before me. She smiled patiently.

'Perhaps ... I'll just have a coffee.'

She turned and left. I was going to call her back to tell her what sort of coffee, but let her go. She brought back the coffee black. I guessed that she wasn't angry with me anymore.

'Sir likes it black?'

'Yes, thank you.'

Our eyes held each other for a moment. She was relaxed. I asked her, without the use of words, whether she would come if I asked her and thought I heard her reply. When she left, I had a sudden feeling of hurt deep within me. I remembered all those years of waiting and that I should find someone now, so exquisite, so eternal, now, when I had the scars of so much that I had missed or lost. I wondered whether her youth would be blind enough to see me as if I were a young man promising her the world rather than one that could give her most of it now. Would she miss the suffering that youth so thrives on or, would she be happy to suffer the anxiety of trying to find new dreams?

The pain reminded me that I was already hoping for something beyond anything I had the right to hope for, but I knew the pain would pass. I watched her, stealing glances whenever I could. I saw her speak to one of the other waitresses and watched them giggle as little girls do in playgrounds about little boys. I wondered whether they might be giggling about me. Embarrassed, I looked away for a moment. Turning back I saw them smiling at me. My embarrassment left me. I looked at my watch. There were thirty-five minutes to go. I signed the

180

bill and nodded goodnight as I left the dining room.

When I got back to my room I felt sick. Everything I stood for stared at me in astonishment. I defended myself as best I could; I didn't care whether I was making a fool of myself, nothing mattered, tomorrow would take care of itself as it always had, so what if nothing came of it, all the constraints I placed on myself never yielded any value so why make the same mistake again. I shaved, showered and changed into a clean shirt. I put on the only jacket I'd brought with me and checked my watch again. I still had fifteen minutes to spare.

The doorman wished me a good evening as I walked out of the hotel and I wished myself a good evening too. The adventure had begun. I remember the sense of excitement I felt. I walked over to the park and sat on a bench hidden behind a tree from the entrance to the hotel. The park lighting was subdued but enough to ward off any unwelcome guests. A few couples in the distance strolled hand in hand while others blessed park benches with desperate promises of love and carelessness. It was crowded enough not to be noticed. I checked my watch. It was time. I waited. I was glad I wore my jacket even though there were others still sporting the flesh of youth in see through t-shirts. I tried to remember whether somewhere in my fading memory I'd been one of them. And then, at first a silhouette then I saw her unmistakable form; a hologram revealing its image.

She crossed the road, unhurried, and walked along the path through manicured gardens that formed oases in the park. I could see her as clearly as I imagined her and wondered whether she could see me. I looked around to see whether anyone else was watching as she walked towards me. I didn't notice anyone. As she followed the path towards me I stood up. I could see her smile. I smiled too with the delight of a sixteen year old.

'You came.'

'Yes. Have you been waiting long?'

I stole an answer from a film I'd seen as a child, 'eternity,' I replied.

'It's late. I have to go home.'

'I know.'

'Why did you want to see me today?'

How do you explain those thoughts that inspire us to do the things we do when there is no rhyme or reason. The cliché doesn't fit. There are so many reasons. How could I explain in the few words of explanation she asked for why I'd taken a chance that any sane person would have told me was pointless and maybe even dangerous?

It had been such a long time since I'd seen anyone who had moved me as she did. In the absence of pure physical desire there exists a nightmare of emotions words cannot explain. I was lifted like the goat following lovers in a Chagall, rude and unkempt, out of place, but necessary. Why a goat? The symbolism seems meaningless when explained compared to the emotion that is aroused when felt, and yet, how can you have a picture like that, about love, without a goat. How do I explain that I'm lost and have been lost for so long that I can't remember how to be found again? How can I tell her, who has seen so little of the life I've journeyed for so long that my feet are numb? Would she understand? Would she spend the rest of her life trying to understand what moves someone like me to fall from grace into her arms?

'So, are you going to say something?'

'I don't know what to say. I can't say why I wanted to see you.'

'Look,' she said irritated by my honesty, 'I'm sorry but I have to go.'

'How do you go home?'

'Well, today I will walk because I have missed the last bus. Chef asked me to help him so I had to stay.'

'Can I walk with you?'

She laughed. 'Do you know how far it is?'

'Further than a life time?'

'You're a funny man. I don't understand you, but you can walk with me if you like.'

And so we walked through the night, through parks that filled me with fear, but clearly familiar to her. It was a long walk. We talked of her work, her family, her town all those miles away that I hadn't heard of, and still we walked. She told me of her friends, her last boyfriend, and how he'd left her for a girl that owned her own flat.

When we arrived at her block of flats I think there was a moment of hesitation for both of us, but she showed courage.

I followed her in silence through a dark passage, up darker stairs to the fourth or fifth floor, and along a corridor lit by the night sky looking in through a window. She stopped at a door without a number, fumbled for a set of keys and opened it switching on the light as she went in. I followed her into a little room with a sink and a bed, and noticed, as I shut the door behind me, clothes hung on the back of the door. It was a tidy flat not normally associated with a young girl living on her own. Everything; clothes, shoes, bags and hats, all kept out of the way.

She switched on a radio and went into a kitchen no larger than a cupboard to make some tea. I marvelled at the economical use of space. As she made the tea she told me that no one had ever listened to her speak for such a long time as I had. I smiled at the compliment saying she sang like a sparrow. She asked me whether sparrows sing. I didn't know. The reality of what was happening dawned on me. I wondered what I was doing there and apologised for keeping her up especially as she had to go to work the next day. She sniggered reminding me she'd already told me tomorrow was her day off. She would get up late and do the washing, buy some groceries and clean the flat. She told me how she missed her little town where her brothers and sisters still played and her parents complained that she didn't send enough money home. I listened, enrapt in the musical symphony of the spheres until Jupiter sprung as Holst intended, powerful and solemn, and bid me rise.

I got up saying I had to go. She looked confused. I took my chance and asked if, as a parting gift, she would give me a kiss. She said 'no' looking down at her hands.

'I didn't expect that of you,' she said.

I turned to the door to leave.

She asked me to wait while she put on her coat. She said that I was a stranger and she

184

would show me the way back. She said the hotel wasn't far, that she'd taken a long way home.

She took my arm as we walked back and I felt the warmth of her pity. We didn't say anything on the walk back, each caught in an entangled web that strangled speech. Confused, exhausted, we finally arrived. She let go of my arm as we got near the hotel and said goodnight. I said goodnight too and turned to leave her behind. As I was about to walk away she grabbed my arm, pulled me gently towards her and kissed me. It was a long and tender kiss. I marvelled at the exploration of her tongue. I embraced her in the name of all loves lost. She waited for me to release her. Mortal though she was, she became my eternity. Blonde hair sparkling in the street lights around a face as pale as fate, lips that you could only ever dream of, all there held in the cup of my hands. I felt a sharp pain in my chest as I let her go.

'I'm sorry,' she said.

I replied with the smile of a weary traveller that had just found out the reality of another mirage, turned and crossed the street to the hotel.

♪♪♪

I thought of her the next day while Ian told me what a wonderful job I'd done and how sorry he was to see me go. The paper couldn't afford two reporters on the same job. He said I must be pleased that I'd been given an assignment in Paris. I didn't care. There was nothing left for me to do. I said I wasn't well and

185

stayed in my hotel room. I'd felt like that once before, a long time ago.

I packed my things ready to leave. It was an early morning flight and I wouldn't have time for breakfast even if I'd wanted it.

I slept a dreamless sleep waking to an alarm that still had my body aching for rest. Numb, I went through the motions of washing and getting ready for that long journey home, wherever that may be.

As I opened the door to my hotel room I saw a rose on the floor. A red rose still in its bud. No note, just the rose. The flower held tightly in the green leaves that would never open. I picked up the rose and a thorn pierced my skin. The drop of blood ballooned and dripped onto the rose as I felt the sweet pain of life passing me by.

*   *   *

The New Faith

J

I noticed her about half an hour ago. She looked disinterested enough in what was going on around her which suggested she wasn't waiting for anyone. It wasn't the first time I'd seen her. I was on my own too and, not looking forward to spending the rest of the evening with my beer, I decided to walk up to her.

'Hi,' I smile.

The blank expression she greets me with gives me the impression she's sizing me up. A moment or two later her face relaxes and she acknowledges me as one would a stranger.

'How are you?'

There is a pause while she thinks about whether or not she wants to respond.

'Ok,' she says, turning back to her drink.

'Hmm, Ok, as in 'I'm feeling great' or 'Ok as things go, yuck! Shit happens right, and you don't want to really know how I feel.'

'Ok, yuck!' She smiles as she says it and I'm happy I've made contact. She wasn't someone I'd have picked for company given a choice, but I think life's about making the best of what you've got.

She turns back to her drink again and I look around me for inspiration. We are surrounded by couples huddled on sofas or tables for two; escapees from bedsits with dying televisions that have given up trying to entertain

187

or, kitchenettes with microwaves providing TV meals for two.

'So, do you come here often?'

'Why do you want to know?'

'I don't know. I'm just making conversation.'

I turn to my beer which is bored and getting flatter by the minute. Maybe she's not bad looking. Maybe I would've picked her if I had a choice. Pity she doesn't want to make conversation. I take a swig of my beer feeling the bubbles rise up my nose, realising, as I do so, I've gulped down too many bubbles and, in a minute I'm going to burp. I wait purposefully, looking away from her. I burp quietly with as much dignity as I can muster.

The bar plays a reggae sound of a nondescript era; probably post Marley, before rap became the emblem of black 'with it' kids. No-one listens to the words as the singer cries into marijuana smoke about the lost faith.

I found myself facing her again. The thirty seconds that have passed since the last exchange mellowed the contortions of a face that once was. I fancied the sighting of a smile and smiled back.

'I'm sorry,' I said.

'That's ok.'

'I just thought that rather than both of us sit here on our own we might pass the time in conversation.'

'That's ok. I didn't understand.'

'No, neither did I. Don't worry, it doesn't matter. Life is about accumulating misunderstandings.'

'You're quite the philosopher.'

188

I smile in surrender.

I've begun to hear myself speak and that's a bad sign. I've been trying to stop speaking just before revealing the miserable bastard I've become, a font of all knowledge that has no use beyond boring the pants off people.

A man walks in. He has one arm. I've seen him before, too. He will buy a drink and sit down with a smile surveying all those around him, hoping no doubt that someone will notice him. He reminds me.

'Do you come here often?'

'You asked me that before.'

'I know, but you didn't answer the question'.

'Does it matter?'

I'm caught off guard. Where looks didn't entice me, conversation is beginning to. Unsure about what to say, I think maybe I should stop before I end up where I've been. I remember the man with one arm and I don't want to be like that while there's still a chance of becoming something more; maybe not loved, but at least someone who's escaped the loneliness of being on his own.

'Is it possible to start again?' I ask.

'Maybe.'

I thank her and turn to my beer for inspiration.

JJ

I was on the tube. Quietly observing those around me, ears plugs in place but my iPod switched off to avoid suffering complaining

189

passengers tut tutting at my selfishness. Not that I should have bothered because they still gave me the same looks they would've done had it been switched on.

There were a group of friends, three lads not long out of school and not long enough in employment to have their brashness knocked out of them. They were laughing at 'in jokes' in a language of single syllables. A girl got on waving a reluctant good-bye. It was still early and she could have missed the tube if she'd wanted to. The tube left the station and she looked around for a suitable seat. She picked one next to the group of friends. She concentrated on the mantra of ego; trying to attract attention, at the same time giving the impression she didn't really care. It didn't matter that the boys weren't interested.

An old woman sitting opposite me looked at my headphones, ignored me and, instead, picked on the lady sitting with shopping bags across the empty aisle.

'You should be careful with your bags.'

No reaction.

'I said, you should be careful,' she repeated a little louder, 'there are a lot of thieves about.'

It took a moment before the other passenger realised she was being spoken to.

'Sorry?' she asked, falling into the trap that only the well healed like myself know how to avoid.

'I said. You should be careful about your bags. I had my bags stolen once. Young people don't have any respect anymore.'

'Thanks, I will.'

'No, I really mean it. It doesn't take a minute.'

The passenger with the shopping bags finally got the message and, ignoring her, looked the other way. The old lady was now talking to herself. She emptied two or three more sentences, mercifully drowned by the sound of the tube taking us beyond the present, until she too realised she'd lost her audience.

The tube screeched to a halt, the doors flung open and more unsuspecting souls poured in. The old lady moved across the aisle providing gender symmetry to the unevenness created by the girl with the affected good-bye wave. The carriage filled up, but still left empty aisles to be talked across.

The doors slammed shut with a warning thud and the tube jolted into movement. I noticed the girl still sitting smug in the centre of her imaginary attention. I allowed her the conceit as a legacy of the effort made in planning for her date which evidently had been a success. She could go home in the knowledge that, having saved herself, she could look forward to another one with certainty.

'You know you should be careful.'

This time the victim was a young man holding his wallet in his hands. I wondered how much research had been required to determine the propensity human beings have to being vulnerable to theft. I suppose the young man was asking for it.

'You shouldn't hold your wallet like that. Thieves will notice it and you could lose it.'

'Don't worry about it.'

'But I do. It happened to me once.'

191

The tube was hurtling along in full flow, making as much noise as it could to save the old lady from more embarrassment. I heard the friends laugh at her. This time there was no 'in joke' necessary to give them a reason to laugh; the old lady had been good enough to provide it. The young man ignored her with politeness.

At the next stop the lady left the carriage. I was glad. Something of the latent humanity my university had left me allowed me to see the old woman as a victim that had been spared more humiliation. My gratitude to the gods that look after the old was short-lived as I saw her enter the next carriage of unwilling prey.

♩♩♩

The man with one arm was still there, sitting in the centre of the wine bar enjoying the increasing volume of conversation around him and practicing his ability of not making eye contact with anyone.

'Thank you,' I said to the girl, 'I accept your offer of 'maybe' as good enough. I'll start again.'

I looked away from her to get into character and then turned back to face her.

'Hello,' I smiled.

In the interlude the music had become louder encouraging raucous conversation where alcohol was slow to help.

'I noticed you sitting on your own.' I paused. 'Are you waiting for someone?'

'The first part was ok,' she said, 'delete the question and don't ask me what I do for a living or whether I'm married?'

Ok, I thought. What she did for a living intrigued me but the marriage part didn't. I'm not blind; the wedding band biting into the flesh of her tell-tale finger answered that question. The fact she was sitting on her own told me she wasn't a newlywed.

'Do you come here often?'

'Sometimes.'

I wanted to ask why she came, where her husband was, what she did for a living...why didn't she want me to ask her what she did for a living.

She wasn't someone I could be desperate about, or was she? Actually, she was nobody, one that couldn't demand much attention other than from someone like me. How desperate was she?

I took another sip and looked around. Everyone was engaged in some activity and the noise of conversation and the music competed for attention. I decided it was too much for me to concentrate on what I was doing. I shut my eyes and imagined everyone disappear into the darkness of the night. I opened my eyes and turned to see her staring into the crowd as I drove them out of the wine bar.

'Can I join you?'

She turned to me slowly. It was deliberate. She looked at the empty chair and then at me.

'If you want to.'

I got up, moved across the two feet that separated us, moved the extra chair away to ward off intruders, and sat down.

$\mathcal{SV}$

I was cycling back from the park. It was hot and I had nowhere to go. I imagined an empty flat and delayed the experience that awaited me by stopping for an ice-cream. I chained the bike to railings before buying myself an ice-cream from a hole-in-the-wall. There were tables and chairs set outside the hole-in-the-wall counter and I sat down at a table that was free. There was nothing much out of the ordinary to look at, just a few people relying on drinks to relieve them from the heat. On a table nearby was an old lady dressed in a pre-war statement of misplaced elegance. I noticed her because of the oddness of her clothes, wondering how she coped with the heat others were still suffering despite being stripped down to 'beach wear'.

I licked my ice-cream with the attention it deserved. I noticed her again. This time our eyes met. I noticed her smile as I looked away hoping she would believe I hadn't noticed her.

'Hello.'

I looked up and saw her standing in front of me.

'Would you like a biscuit,' she said, offering me a grease stained, brown paper bag. 'They're fresh. I baked them myself.'

'No thanks.' I smiled with politeness.

'Can I sit down?' She didn't wait for me to answer, pulled up a chair and sat down.

'Where are you from?'

It was a strange question but the colour of my skin still encouraged such questions from a generation that hadn't accepted the legacy of mass immigration. I ignored her question.

'Please don't be angry. I don't want to trouble you. I just want to be friendly.'

I suffered a pang of guilt and smiled an apology.

'I'm sorry. I'm not angry. I'm waiting for someone.' I lied.

'It is very hot today.'

'Yes,' I said, looking round to see whether anyone else had noticed the old lady come and sit with me. I wanted her to go away, but didn't know how to ask her to leave. I wondered why the old demand respect; was it for their vulnerability or, was it because they reminded us of parents, guilt ridden, we'd left behind or, who had died providing us with the opportunity of remembering them with affection.

'I don't want to bother you.'

'No, you're not bothering me,' I lied, again.

'I'm all alone,' she said, 'all I want is someone to talk to.'

I faked a smile to hide my disgust. This is why society demands old people's homes or hospices for the terminally ill. Like leper colonies, they're kept away from us so that we're not reminded of our eventual passing to the other side. Disabilities are best confined to charity boxes chained outside shops, or collection boxes that sit beside tills in which the one penny change is left to ease our consciences for committing the sin of indulgence.

195

'It is hot,' I said.

'I know. I wish I were dead.'

The statement was out of context. I'd lost my parents, both of whom had struggled humiliatingly trying to avoid the call of death and, here was an old hag, much older and still alive, who wanted to die.

'You shouldn't say that. There're many people fighting to live and you have everything.'

'No, son, I don't have anything. My friends have all died. I have a sister who will not speak to me and I have nothing to do.'

I could see tears welling in her eyes. I knew it was time to leave. The ice-cream was almost done. I threw the rest of it away.

'Are you alone?' she asked.

I got up and left.

'I've seen you here before.'

'Yes, I've seen you too. I've wondered what a beautiful woman like you is doing sitting all on her own.'

She smiled. I hadn't stopped smiling. I felt a glimmer of hope. Hope for what, I wasn't sure, but it felt a lot better than I'd been feeling a few minutes ago.

'It's hot.'

'Yes.'

'I wanted to ask you all the usual questions but you stopped me.'

'I know. They're so boring. It's almost as if everyone needs to put us into a familiar box before any social interaction can take place.'

I thought about what she was saying. She looked as if she knew I was struggling again.

'So, what did you want to know about me,' she asked.

'I don't know...what, for instance, you do for a living.'

'I'm a prostitute!'

I laughed half out of embarrassment and half at the ridiculousness of her answer.

'OK, I won't ask the question.'

'Good.'

I looked around to see whether anyone had heard. Nobody.

'I see you want to be left on your own.'

'You've said that already.'

'Do you want to be left on your own?'

She looked away. I waited. She still looked away.

I got up and left. As I was walked out of the wine bar someone came up behind me and tapped me on the shoulder. It was the waiter.

'I'm sorry sir, your bill?'

I apologised and paid. I noticed her through the window still looking away. She didn't care. I didn't care either. It was just one of those situations in which we find ourselves until I lose an arm and she waits to die.

*　　*　　*

Times Past
& Future Meetings

J

It wasn't always like this, or was it? Is it memory that plays tricks on us or, does the present prevent us remembering the past? Were you the one that enticed me with the desire to be with you once upon a time? I seem to remember in the distant past, when life was full of hope for something I was conditioned to want and, believing I'd found it, I worked through the tortuous beginnings of a relationship. By the time I'd persuaded you that I was worth taking a chance on I was exhausted. Then you took over until, sated with the pleasure and promise of the relationship we thought we once had, we left each other to find something new.

Sitting in the park, looking back, I remember that it wasn't always like this. I don't want my memories to be like this. I want them to be like those of couples lying on the grass, looking at clouds, being themselves, talking about nothing that matters, and yet, that is all that matters; the most precious pleasure that we can ever have.

When we decided to go our own separate ways, I threw away all the photographs I had of you, except one, which I hid. I never looked at it for all the time we were apart and then, when after all those years I saw you again, I spent a whole afternoon looking for it. It wasn't until a lot later that I found it. Until I found it, I thought you hadn't changed. Your voice sounded familiar, your hair fell as I remembered it and, apart from a little tiredness around your eyes, I thought I saw something you had when I first loved you, or, was it when we loved each other? I can't remember.

Neither of us had anywhere to go, just as it had been when we first met. The dreams of childhood that maturity destroyed, left us both too tired to recreate what we knew was lost.

I don't how it is in a city of eight million people that fate allows the chance meeting of people like us.

♩♩

I was coming in to London which was rare. A familiar voice on the train answering a telephone call distracted me from the book I was reading and, although I didn't turn around, I listened to your voice as I would an old song I hadn't heard in a long time. The trains are a lot quieter now for which I'm grateful. I tried to remember where it was I'd heard that voice. I would like to say I recognised it immediately, but then, we're past lying. That's what disappointment does to you, or is it experience?

You left a long time ago. I mean we left each other a long time ago. There were no references that allowed me to remember specifically what was so familiar, but there was something.

After you'd finished the call I turned to the book I was reading, quietly regretting the

199

choice I'd made for the journey. Thankfully, it was not long before the train, tired of travelling sped through the last few stations before it entered with a familiar screech into the cavernous echo of Victoria station. I waited for the others to get off the train. The others had a pressing need to get to where they were going. We both must have had the same idea because, as chance would have it, we stood facing each other just as we were about to step off the train. Perhaps it was the surprise of seeing each other again or, maybe the fact that after all those years we recognised each other that left us struggling to say something. The welling up of words failing to engage sound left us in silence. The crowds encouraged us to step off the train and, the few moments it took to find a place to stand on the platform, out of the way of the other passengers, allowed us to gather our thoughts.

'Hello.'

'Hello.'

'It's been a long time.'

'Yes.'

'How are you?'

'Fine, you?'

'Fine.'

'Are you rushing off somewhere?'

'Yes.'

'OK, well, take care.'

'Yes, you too.'

I turned and walked away. I don't know why. It was nice to see you again, but you had your life to live and I suppose I had mine. A chance meeting didn't seem to be enough to set aside our immediate plans. As I passed through the ticket barrier it took me a few moments to find you in the crowd. I saw you look in my direction. If you hadn't looked back I'd have missed you. You waited for me to catch up. Was that what made me walk up to you, you waiting? Maybe it was, or maybe I want you to share in the conspiracy.

'Hi.'

'Hi,' I said.

'Strange us meeting like this.'

'Yes.'

'Do you think it might be worth having a coffee sometime?'

'Yes.'

'What time are you going back?'

'I'm catching the six-fifty two to Dorking,' I replied.

'Shall we meet at six then.'

'OK.'

'Here.'

'OK.'

And that's how it was. Fifteen years of wasteland crossed in a chance meeting and nine hours. You missed the six-fifty two and gave us an extra hour, an extra hour to launder fifteen years. But things don't quite work like that. No amount of recollection is enough to bring back lost time.

I wonder whether it was lost time or, was it time spent reconciling our existence with the present. We had moved away from plans for the good life that never came because we couldn't understand why we ended up together in the first place.

We used the hour to decide whether we wanted to meet up again. The conversations were hard. I had no interest in what you had

201

been up to for fear of realising the reasons I'd made up while we were apart might not be true.

I answered your questions with brevity as you pried. It wasn't that I didn't want to answer your questions but I didn't have much to say. The past had been a collection of good times and bad, as I suspect, is the case for most, with nothing significant to show for it. Through relationships that had come and gone I'd learned to live with the belief that nothing is permanent. I'd hoped to realise that when you died, but didn't wish for an early death.

You thought the reluctance to answer your questions was because I was still hurt. Maybe you're right. It is, after all, romantic to think that the parting of two people joined together by routine and familiarity is so painful that the memory of it can last forever. I know having agreed to meet you I spent the day wondering what there was to talk about. I thought about how easily we could fall into the trap of hurting each other with stories of good times only experienced because we had gone our separate ways or worse; blame. Lonely memories are hard to share.

I tried to think of reasons for not turning up, but told myself that would be selfish. I reminded myself of the hate I felt for you, the disgust I felt for having been so gullible to have believed in love, and blamed you for all the false starts I'd had after you left.

I should have been sad that you were all alone, but that would have been a lie. It gave me satisfaction to hear that you too had not gained anymore than I, and the cruelty of that satisfaction I accentuated by affecting concern. Am I ashamed? No, because I was alone too.

I think if you had not been alone I would have wished it. I think you waited for me to ask you what had happened in the fifteen years of silence; of relationships that hadn't worked out, the pain of loss that you'd felt, but I was content to hear of your work and where you lived; of the loss of your parents and indulge you in the sadness of not being able to have children. I think I felt sorry for us, not you, when I showed sympathy. I felt sorry for the loss we'd endured because of the childish exuberance with which we had ventured out of our relationship in search of something new.

There is nothing new about wanting to find something more than you have. We do it all the time, as if what we have was too easily had. The excitement of the struggle, when we're not engaged in it, is too hard to resist. I'm not sure that's true, but somehow I've become desperate to find such universal truths.

We'd agreed to live apart for a while to help us understand our relationship. We needed proof we were in love. I happily played along although, as time passed, I began to enjoy playing the role of victim and played it well, until I found it infertile for new relationships. You moved away which made it easier for us. You didn't call. I was glad there were no messages to ignore. It was hard at first, but I soon found a lost tribe of lonely souls and enjoyed being at one with them. I found bars for people learning to be single again, and enjoyed the hangovers in penance for worshiping Bacchus. Thus cleansed, I became human enough to pass my days in

203

normal company. In the evening the addiction was hard to control. And then, tired of running, one evening I found Evelyn, auburn haired Evelyn, who shared my evenings and allowed me nights out with the boys until the children came. Two boys that would have grown up to be my proud sons had Evelyn not taken them away from me; Evelyn who I loved more in death than I had ever loved in life. My years were spent in mourning. I was lucky to have fate to blame. Evelyn replaced your memory and my boys consumed my love. Three bodies, cold to the touch, were all I wanted to remember. I had no need of you. I chose the cold white marble angels that stand in silence on either side of Evelyn. And in that silence that I'd become accustomed to, for no earthly reason, in a city of eight million people, we found each other.

We met again and traded stories told with embellishment as the memory of them moved us. We remembered old times through the few photographs we hadn't destroyed, as if the distance we'd covered could be ignored or, argued to have been an experience worth having.

A photograph of you looking over my shoulder sits on the bedside table. We laughed that sun drenched day. It sits beside creams and lotions that promise to bring back our youth, but there's no disguise for the smell of age.

You snore unashamedly now as I sit and watch the heaving of your flesh with cruelty. We made love as if somehow the sweat, the exertion, and false promises could bring back all we've lost. I try to remember that it wasn't like this, or...maybe it was.

*   *   *

Good-bye to all that

J

The justice of Solomon seeks truth through an emotional bond that is greater than the desire of possession and yet, how much did he love to let Sheba go. Three years of love that went beyond the responsibilities of being a queen, the birth of a son and that was it until she died.

There is something to be said for the love of doing what is right, but then, I always wonder to what extent passion has a role to play in determining why we always look for something more than we know to be right. We spend so much of our lives debating the virtue of right over wrong, and yet, the confessional sees us seek absolution for misdemeanours that we happily commit expecting a forgiving God to save us from the consequences. The lucky among us are happy to live our lives believing that to stray from the true path, temporarily, deserves forgiveness and, at the same time, look down on those who take one step too many, believing that, no matter what the consequences, it can't be worth it. No temporary delusion, but a permanent step that no number of 'Hail Mary's' would allow us back into a state of grace. What would we have said if Sheba had stayed, or if Solomon had left for love?

33

He was a friend who deserved to be my friend because of the admiration I had for him. I knew from the first time I met him that I was in the presence of someone stronger than I had any hope of becoming, and wiser than I had the courage to become. He was a man who I determined to endow with virtues beyond those any normal man could have because he was an ordinary human being, not one blessed with powers reserved for those who walk in the grace of God. Those, one can only revere, not emulate, because they are blessed with living in what I can only describe as a dimension beyond our earthly existence. I know, by saying this, I'm accepting my own failure as a sinner, but the written word has to begin with truth if it is worth writing.

Giles had been a man who had, after a rebellious youth, turned to living a life most men and women envy. Success in education came only when most of his peers had long ended their penance of speaking with words others had written. Giles had managed to complete a classics degree with a first. The myth of sex, drugs and rock and roll had been discredited. His choice of subject to study as a mature student had been more of a surprise to his disillusioned parents than his earlier dropping out of school.

His father, moderately rich and successful, as he often liked to remind his family, had despaired of his only son from an early age and, although he would not have admitted it to his wife, he was glad when Giles left home, sparing him the disruption to domestic bliss that throwing him out would have caused. Of course, his mother was devastated and his father comforted her by sharing the self pity she enjoyed.

They were intelligent people and, using that intelligence, were able to persuade themselves that it wasn't through any fault of their own that their son had turned out the way he had, but instead, an unfortunate consequence of changing times. They knew that anything else would have jeopardised the comfortable middle class life they'd spent the best years of their lives achieving and, having made it, were happy to live the rest of their lives in the fear of losing it.

When I first met Giles he was already reformed. His crisp appearance, as well as that of his wife, became the subject of conversation on the drive home from the party. He was guest of honour and Steven, an old school friend, had been delighted to show him off. Mary, my wife, decided that his wife wasn't good enough for Giles.

She was elegant and, the two children they had, had not affected her sexuality. Still in her late thirties she dressed in a way that left no doubt to onlookers that she knew her husband needed to be attracted by her and, that attraction, had to be more than familiarity or convenience. Tall enough for Giles, who was not tall, and bronzed lightly enough for the tan to appear real, with hair that fell onto her shoulders with the delight of being free from shampoos, gels and sprays, in as natural a blonde as could be had without being suspected. She carried herself well, in my view, with the flair of accustomed good living in the knowledge that everyone around her understood the deference she deserved. Mary thought that she wasn't living up to the position marriage to Giles offered her and, that she should have tried harder. 'How?', if I'd asked the question, would only have caused a row to hide the fact that she couldn't say.

Giles and I became friends. The common interest in squash helped. He was a lot better than I was, but never made me feel inadequate. On the contrary, he often remarked that playing with me demonstrated that sports didn't have to be so competitive so as to make one forget that friendship requires gentle handling of emotions and compromise. His wisdom, that is all I can call it, inspired me. I learned from him, enjoyed his company, relaxed with him and, throughout the twenty or so years that I knew him before he retired, never once felt other than his equal.

He retired early. His wife asked for a divorce two years earlier and, the settlement she got was not begrudged by him. Divorce is rarely, if ever, not acrimonious and theirs had its moments. The children had left home starting their own lives at different ends of the country, depriving her of the solace of supporters, which she believed they would have been if they'd lived closer.

I remember when it started. We had just finished a game of squash which I had won easily, which was unusual, although I didn't think it at the time. Giles asked if I minded not playing another game. I was happy to stop on a winning streak.

'Are you alright, Giles?'

'Yes, fine Mark. I suppose I still haven't gotten over the jet-lag.'

'Where was it this time?'

'Hong Kong.'

'It's supposed to take an hour a day to get over it, isn't it?'

'Yes, normally.'

It was an opening that I took without any real curiosity. I knew he had been on a trip to see a client and had extended his trip at the clients' invitation to see the Great Wall of China.

'So did you at least take some photographs?'

'No.' There was a pause. 'I didn't go.'

'I thought you told Mary that you did. She said after speaking to you how she envied you and how miserable you were for not taking Helen with you.'

'Yes, well, Helen thinks I went too.'

'Come on Giles, the suspense is killing me. What have you been up to?' and this is what he told me.

He went to Hong Kong. That part of it happened. The client was planning the trip to the Great Wall and, at the very last minute, suggested they fly to Bangkok instead. Giles, even though he knew what was on offer, agreed. They spent three days and nights drinking in the company of prostitutes and getting very little sleep.

Our friendship had long passed the boundaries where either of us would invoke the hypocrisy of moral indignation and, although I

209

had not indulged in similar escapades, I was honest enough to admit that it was more for lack of opportunity than any sense of propriety. He told me of their eagerness to please and, putting aside the health risks that publicity would encourage me to fear, I listened with salacious envy.

'Oh well,' I said, 'that's another memory that you can lock away to look back on.'

'Mark, that's not the end of it. It was so fantastic that I can't wait to go again.'

It was then that I felt a desire to give him some advice.

'Don't be silly, Giles. Once is what you can be lucky enough to get away with. Repeating something like that is tempting providence.'

He didn't respond and I didn't press him. We went home and the subject never came up until about three months later when he told me that he was going off again, this time to Kuala Lumpur. I don't know why it occurred to me to ask him, but I knew the answer before he told me.

'Yes, I'm flying to Bangkok.'

'Giles, be careful. You have a lot to lose. I know it is high time that we had our obligatory mid-life crisis, but why don't you get an Aston Martin or something? It's a lot safer and, in the long run, all you risk is an expensive hobby.'

'You do that Mark. Somehow that's not enough for me. What am I going to do driving around in an Aston anyhow? I don't have a need to show anyone that I've made it. It doesn't mean anything, anyway.

The vehemence of his conviction seemed more emotional than was appropriate in the exchange of friendly banter. That night lying in bed, unable to sleep, I still managed to resist the temptation of discussing it with Mary. Instead, I thought about my own life.

I had worked hard which, combined with luck of being in the right place at the right time, had given me the comfort of not knowing what it's like to want something with desperation, the sort of desire that suppresses the fear of losing what you have. I couldn't say that I had everything I ever wanted, but I was content with what I could afford. I fell asleep in the lullaby of Mary's gentle, satisfied, snoring.

I didn't speak to Giles again before he left. Maybe I'd put him off confiding in me because of the unsuccessful attempt at lecturing him. I rang him a week later and was told he was on vacation. He had actually taken three weeks off. I didn't dare think how he had explained this to Helen. After all, no matter how naïve we think them, I find women in general, and wives in particular, not quite the trusting souls we hope they are. I didn't ring Helen and didn't mention it to Mary either. I wanted to talk about it with someone, but kept it to myself. I decided the desperate need to speak to someone was a personal need to justify to myself that what Giles was up to was not only wrong, but he wouldn't get away with it. When I finally managed to speak to him, all I got was an adolescent exuberance of finding the pleasure of sex for the first time.

I think he must have got divorced shortly after that. There were no soul searching conversations with me or any of his friends of which I'm aware. He seemed to have kept it very

211

quiet. They both did. Helen, who we all agreed, had every reason to be upset by the whole affair, also reacted in a way that was very different to how we imagined any wife should. I imagine she was bitter about losing someone she believed would be there to make sure her old age would be bearable, but there was no scandal. I suppose we felt deprived of the soap opera reaction that makes us content with our lot in life. We let it go, agreeing that we always thought they were strange. I did try and call, left a few messages and, when he didn't ring me back, decided he wanted to be left alone.

♪♪♪

It was about two years later that I got a call from him. I had moved on with my life, found another squash partner and although I thought of him from time to time, Giles was filed away as a friend I once had. I don't believe in dragging on a relationship beyond what mutual desire requires. One sided anything is doomed to die and friendship is probably one of the more vulnerable relationships we indulge in.

'Hello Mark, it's Giles.'

His voice took a moment to register.

'Sorry, are you busy.'

'No Giles, I'm sorry. It's been a while. Where are you?'

I heard him laugh as he told me he was still where he'd always been. For a moment I assumed the divorce had been a scare and everything was back to normal.

212

'Thank God, Giles. You gave us such a scare about getting a divorce.'

'We have.'

I was confused and I think Giles sensed it too. He asked whether I had time to meet up for a drink after work which I agreed to do.

There are moments when curiosity captivates us despite the fact that there's nothing to be curious about. In spite of our rational selves we feel desperate to find out what we already know. I was caught in one of those moments. I flatter myself that there were some remnants of our long friendship that encouraged me more than mere curiosity, but that wouldn't be true.

This time I mentioned it to Mary. She dismissed him as someone who didn't matter enough to think about, was surprised I'd agreed to meet him, but didn't care if I did. Mary was like that sometimes; confident enough to ignore me as if I were a teenage child who wanted to do something that didn't matter in the great scheme of things.

I met Giles at a bar near Paddington station after work. He looked well. He'd aged a little. He met me as if he was meeting me after a week rather than after almost two years. There was no great display you would imagine of long lost friends meeting again. It was almost casual and I soon forgot that any time had elapsed since we last met.

He ordered me a drink, asked how I was, what I was up to and listened as Giles always did. I surprised myself at the matter of factness at which I told him about Mary having a stroke, but recovering, the children all at university and

213

changes at work that had made me start thinking about early retirement.

'Well, that's me, Giles. What about you?'

'Not as exciting as you. I've sold up, settled with Helen, bought a place in Bangkok and am moving next week.'

There was a moment of stunned silence before we both burst out laughing.

I haven't seen him since, but still often think of the foolishness of middle age that makes us do things we can't explain. Words, I suppose, aren't enough.

* * *